Sky
Almighty!

Two Trolley Dollies

Telling Tales

A Novel

by

Franco Lombini & Mario Tadiello

La Gedeona Press

Sky Almighty!

Two Trolley Dollies Telling Tales

Franco Lombini & Mario Tadiello

franco.lombini@icloud.com

mariotadiello@outlook.it

ISBN 978-1-80049-160-1

To Gedeone who listened to our stories

without batting a whisker

from under the rhubarb

in our cottage garden

To Ercole, Paride, and Ettore

who baaed their way

into our lives

And to Giuliana who taught us

the importance of carpe diem

with a flap of her wings

0

Taxing out

A life spent burning the midnight oil.

Stewards.

Stewardesses.

Cabin crew.

Flight attendants.

Trolley Dollies.

One job… so many names, so many stories, so many clichés, so many sleepless nights… so many passengers!

"They look so gorgeous in their uniform! Always immaculate! It's so lovely to see them walking thorough the airport. I feel safe just by watching them. So elegant…"

You should see me after a little present from a passenger who has forgotten to take her tablets for motion sickness.

"I've always wondered… Do pilots marry stewardesses? How can they manage otherwise? They are always away!"

So, what's left for stewards… fairies?

"At the end of the day, they are just waiters in the sky."

As far as I know, at The Ritz, they don't have bunks, kamikazes and handcuffs... but they do get tips though!

"I don't think they have a house. Renting one would be a waste of money while buying it wouldn't make any sense at all! It would get old without being used. Besides, I don't even know if they can get a mortgage..."

Praised be the Lord for the last instalment!

"Would you believe it? They can't even donate their organs!"

We can't give blood either, for that matter!

"How do they cope with kids?"

Folding children in a suitcase is indeed an extremely complicated business, but it can be done!

Cabin crew. So many stories have been told about us! How many of these are a figment of wannabe aviators or passengers' troubled minds and how many are true or even vaguely resembling reality?

Lo and behold, this is showdown time! The chips are down, *we* are holding the life jacket toggle! Time to get even and fill that 'air pocket' that all too often goes under the radar. What do passengers do onboard long-haul flights? And why? And if at that altitude they still know what they are doing, will there be Someone willing to forgive their actions and trespasses?

One thing is for sure, in the highest heavens, reality far exceeds any earthly imagination and this time it won't be boring and lazy pub tales spread by passengers – kings and queens for a night - but confessions from two horses' mouths, two mouthy bewildered stewards sharing what they see and hear flight in flight out.

Thus, fasten your seatbelt and get ready for take-off. We will take you on an around-the-world discovery voyage into human turbulence: fifty short stories where the only moral is the madness set off by hypoxia, where anything is allowed, where nobody knows anybody, in no-man's airspace, where tomorrow is another day, and the sky is the only limit.

1

Top Ten

Here we go again, same old story! The overbooking phenomenon strikes back! Out of the 54 passengers in Business Class, 20 are full-fare customers, whilst the rest have all been upgraded. In 'plane' English, more bums than seats in Economy Class. That would not be much of a problem, if it weren't for the fact that many of the blessed have unrealistic, futuristic and, let's be honest, compulsive expectations.

As if we didn't know that they are mere Business parvenus. The passenger list shows the profile of every single customer. We even know if we are to keep a safe distance from those with halitosis, better known in Economy as bad breath. The ground staff are unforgivably ruthless in their final evaluation.

Anyhow, on the Miami-London leg, here are our top ten (in random order) pearls of wisdom of passengers in Business Class by the skin of their teeth. Indulge yourself at will in creating your own personal favourite chart!

Ready, steady, go!

Case 1

"Can I have a glass of blue champagne, pleaZe?"

"Madam, we've got Taittinger or Rosé Champagne. Regrettably, we don't carry a drop of Blue Champagne on board, I'm afraid!"

"Oh, I saw it in a movie, I thought you might have it."

What film did she see? 'Airplane!'?

Case 2

"The light in the restroom won't turn on, can you help?"

The wardrobe is not illuminated, Sir.

Get out of there or you'll get hurt.

And there's no flush either by the way!

Case 3

"I would like a glass of pink champagne and I'm going to drink it French style. Would you be so kind as to put two ice cubes and one peppercorn?"

Oh là là! French Overseas Territories… what a mess!

Case 4

"We would like two glasses of boiled water… cooled."

Harder by the minute.

"Can I offer it to you straight from the bottle at room temperature?"

"Absolutely not! We are from India; we are used to the pure water of the Himalaya. Have you got a thermometer?"

How come that every time I go to India, the mere thought of opening a tap gives me diarrhoea? It must all boil down to the pure water of the Himalaya, surely.

Ayurveda will save the world, one glass at a time.

Case 5

"When is the Captain coming to see us?"

It ain't a cruise liner, love!

The only occasion when you will ever see the captain strolling down the aisle of an aircraft is when the food didn't agree with their stomach and they don't want to turn the flight deck into a gas chamber. Do not stop them, let them pass through…as quickly as possible.

Case 6

"Nothing for me, thanks."

"Darling, you must try something, for God's sake."

"Honestly, I'm not thirsty."

"Come on, honey bunch! When will you get such an opportunity again?"

"Go on then, order something special. Surprise me!"

"A Coca-Cola… with ice… and… lemon."

Aw! The chance of a lifetime: A Coca-Cola in Business Class is just something else.

Case 7

"Is this the rainbow zone?"

"What do you mean, madam?"

"20E and F. Even our gay friends booked these seats on their flight to Hong Kong. They told us they are very comfy and... private. Thanx."

Crikey, I can see the spark of conception in their eyes but what's in their mind?

Case 8

"For me, a medium size please. I've already got my slippers."

You misinformed! We provide pyjamas only for our First Class passengers... And by the way, do you bring your own slippers before even knowing if you might be upgraded? What about if they don't match?

Case 9

"If you have finished with your starter, Sir, let me take your plate."

"Oh, but I have already eaten my crème caramel… why, was there something else?"

"Yes, your hot entrée is on its way."

"Alright then, so I would like beef, but then I will have to have another dessert… otherwise I feel… as if I was doing everything the wrong way around."

You cheeky glutton! Just tell me you want two desserts. End of story!

Case 10

"What button should I press to rotate my flat-bed chair?"

This is NOT 'The Voice' and I am not Jennifer Hudson.

2

Women on the Verge

"Is the flight full today?"

"Yes, madam."

"I mean, are all these empty seats going to be occupied?"

"Yes, madam, once boarding is complete, it's going to be chock-a-block."

"I don't know whether I'd be able cope with it. Could you bring me a cup of tea whilst I think about it?"

I head for the galley, but I keep watching her, suspiciously, out of the corner of my eye. Too late, they are already too deep; two fingers down anybody's throat can do a lot of damage.

Six seats. She strafed six. A fire hydrant.

"See what happens just at the mere thought of it? Could I just be moved forward to a more comfortable cabin now?"

I inform the cabin manager about the incident. Boarding is now interrupted.

The airside disinfection services come on board with their *The Cassandra Crossing* stage costumes, the rest of the passengers must feel reassured, surely.

"There's a nasty flu around," a few punters comment.

"It's an epidemic."

"And where am I supposed to go in the meantime?" the flooder asks.

"You will have to go through a precautionary disembarkation, madam."

"No way! I must be in Boston by this evening, I have an important dinner; it's extremely important that I should be there! Anyway, I am 'empty', see?" And she starts dry-heaving again with two fingers down her throat. "Even if I wanted to... there's nothing left in me."

No luck, the Cassandra team leaves her on the ground. Next time, she'll think twice before puking her guts out. With the seats all clean as a whistle, boarding is now complete, and off we go.

"Duty free? Gift items? Special offers? Alcohol, tobacco?"

"Yes, I would like that green lipstick that eventually turns red, you know."

"Yes, I am going to get it from First Class for you."

I am about to come back to Economy with my loot, when a lady in her pyjamas greets me with what looks like the Shaka sign. Now, I don't speak sign language, but I have a strong feeling she needs something cylindrical and, since she is vehemently brushing her teeth, I imagine she desperately needs a glass.

I take it to her.

"It just can't be!" she exclaims pressing pause on her video screen.

Well, I must have misinterpreted her gesture. She wanted an inch of whisky, perhaps? She carries on brushing just as passionately.

It must be excellent quality toothpaste. My goodness, I have never seen so much foam in my life!

By the way, I am still holding that glass in case you had forgotten.

"And she is even shagging him!"

Film plots are ever more complicated, I wouldn't know what to add and frankly I can't find any good reason to delve into the subject.

"I've been teaching for over twenty years and I don't think it's fair that such things should happen between teachers and students, what do you think?"

I think it's high time you walked into that toilet, what do you reckon?

A sip of water from the bottle on the table and... and down it goes all the foamy liquid into the glass that I am still holding in one hand, because in the other I am clasping the green lipstick that eventually, if you remember, turns red.

"I think I am a very down to earth person... but, well... no student has ever fallen in love with me, that's the heart of the matter, or a matter of the heart, if you prefer. It depends on the way you look at it. But why?"

I look at her foamy mouth, I glance at the reddish liquid in the glass and everything becomes crystal clear. I am afraid, there is more than one reason why that teacher will stay single for quite a while.

"But I don't want to keep you and I have been terribly rude. I haven't even told you the beginning of the film. Do you mind taking the glass to the toilet? I'm so snug here under the duvet and I really want to see how it all ends."

Before she asks me to immerse her dentures in water, I'd better rush back to Economy; but before that, I mustn't forget to drop her bloody smoothie in the toilet.

3

Orthodox Games

Flight Newark-London, boarding.

"There are 40 of us, all orthodox; have you got our kosher meals?"

We wouldn't even deny them to the 40 thieves.

"Yes, they are all Glatt, don't worry."

"Let's go!" he says, waving his hand to his people while ordering them to board the plane towards the promised meals.

On it comes a gang of boys - with side curls, hatboxes and dressed up in what look like mourning suits - and a bunch of girls - in plain-coloured dresses, flat shoes, 100 denier opaque pantyhose with a back seam highlighting post-pregnancy varicose veins, and lay-sister-style Trevira pleated skirts.

Time is up. The Ark is now closed.

Off we go.

Thy will be done.

Some time later.

"Hello, what's your name?" ask me two children of the Davidic group visibly spiritless.

"Franco, and since I know your next question is going to be if I want to play with you, my answer is 'yes' because everybody is asleep and I am bored to death."

"Yeah! We'll go and fetch our mums' wigs. Don't move!"

And where on earth could I hide?

The two girls come back bouncing up and down with five wigs, no less, which they sneaked off the menorah their mothers had placed on the fold-away table designed for bassinets in the cabin.

"Are you absolutely sure that you have permission to play with these? Are we not going to make your mothers furious and get in trouble?" I ask a little worried.

"Yes, we are allowed. We have no dolls, but we can do what we like with these."

"But why on earth do your mums take their wigs off on board?" I enquire.

"My mum says that she does it because she adores wearing a turban."

"Mine, instead, says that she can't sleep otherwise."

"Wait here, girls, I am going to check the cabin."

Actually, Ruth's daughters are all fast asleep with their heads wrapped up in fine headscarves. I might as well play. I go back to the galley and in the meantime the curly brothers and another nosy child, probably a gentile, have joined the happy gang.

"So, what game are we playing?"

"Well, you are going to be the hairdresser, we brush the wigs then I'll go and fetch the candelabra thingies and we'll hang them, you know, they ain't got seven arms for nothing! You have to guess who they belong to. If you fancy it, you may even shampoo them."

"Deal, only don't cheat, though!"

"No! The blond one is not Sarah's, it's Ruth's, you blockhead!"

I admit it, I have never played *Wigs* before and even at Identikit I have always been a dud.

"Girls, there are too many call bells ringing, I have to go for a juice round in the cabin, they must be parched; how about changing games? Fancy playing air hostesses? You might even wear your beloved wigs. Could you do the last three rows for me, please? I'll get the tray ready for you."

"Yeeeeah!"

"I am not coming," says the gentile girl. "I'd rather stay here watching the wigs; I want to be a *hair* hostess. My mum hasn't got one. I never played combing them; I usually comb the dolls they give me for Christmas. They are a lot nicer!"

OMG! A religious war is about to break out.

"Christmas??? Look, we don't need Christmas presents to have fun."

"Why? Surely, Father Christmas brings you presents too."

"Certainly not, and so what?"

"Girls, come on, let's leave the wigs behind. Sue will stay here on watch, won't you?"

I start the juice round in the cabin, the three Israelite girls do the last three rows for me, the boys stay in the galley playing *Biblicon*, a sort of Millionaire for the few chosen ones, and Sue carries on combing the wigs as if they were Christmas dolls. Perfect, we can all live in harmony after all. Peace be with us.

"Franco, the gentleman in the back row told me I am too noisy and asked me for a 'lesbian tea'. I have never heard of it, what is it?"

"Wait, I'll make one for him. Here you are, you can take it to him now," I say to Esther after giving her a weak tea with milk and lemon for the joker.

"So, who's winning at *Biblicon*?"

"Me! He doesn't even know how old Methuselah was when he died, can you believe it?"

"Well, well, well, and he does not even remember if Judaism has 634 or 645 commandments, how about that?"

"Boys, you are both brilliant. Do you think you can improve your concentration if I bring you the headphones from Business Class?"

I try to keep them entertained with the godly quiz. I must make sure they don't damage their mothers' wigs.

"I can spy with my little eye... something beginning with C... There's a chewing gum in the wig!" Sue shouts radiantly.

Maybe I did not get her properly... has that gentile stuck a gum on a Kosher wig?

"No! My mum is going to hit the roof, because I can play with them, but if shit hits the fan, it's my fault and she's going to punish me for that."

"Language, please! Where did you learn that ugly expression?"

"I heard it from my mum and I asked her what happens when shit accidentally hits a fan, but she wouldn't explain it to me. What's the point in saying something if you don't know what it looks like? That's why I had to find out by myself and thanks to Ralph I did."

"Who's Ralph?"

"My pussy cat. On a hot summer day, we had the fan on in our apartment in Golders Green and Ralph had just gone for a dump in his litter tray. I could not resist it, I had to see what happened, I threw it right at the fan blades. Some of it kind of got stuck in the metal and made a funny noise but most of it got thrown around the room and hit the photo frames on the living room's mantelpiece. What a mess!"

"That's precisely what it means; could you not just take your mum's word for it?"

"Never! She's always taught me that I should not parrot back what I hear in the street, that I should always find things out for myself, so that's what I did."

"Ok, but let's not take it too far today, tell me which wig you stuck it to."

"No way, are you or are you not a hairdresser? Anyway, I didn't do it!"

Bollocks! I now have to comb through all the wigs to try and find the gum before their mums wake up.

"Help me, please. Sue, you go back to your seat now, we won't play with you anymore and I am going to tell on you, and your mum will take care of the rest. I am afraid you won't be having any Christmas presents this year."

"Good!" says Esther, "It serves you right! No wigs and no dolls!"

"Come on, girls, try and find this gum quickly, will you?"

"There it is! But it won't come off!"

"Obviously! How did that rascal manage to squish it like that?"

There's no time to waste, I must fetch the scissors from the medical kit and cut it out. "Rachel, it's the only way, we have to cut a strand, but keep quiet with your mum, she won't even notice. I beg of you!"

"Alright, I trust you, after all you are the hairdresser."

Zack!

"Now go back to your seats and take the 'toys' back into the cabin and let's hope for the best."

Twenty minutes to landing.

I check that everything is ok in the cabin, scowl at Sue who looks at her mum as though butter wouldn't melt in her mouth.

Meanwhile, the wigless take off their turbans and reunite with their fake hairpieces. Their husbands seem to appreciate it, although, deep down, they desire them only purely hairless.

"Mum," says Rachel, "do you know that Franco is a hairdresser?"

"Is that so? Well, in that case he could fix my wig."

Rachel turns around and with one hand on her mouth, leaving a gap between the middle and the ring finger whispers to me, "There's a hole at the back."

"And then he also taught me how to make lesbian tea."

"What?"

It's getting late. I diligently resume my security checks.

Mind that gap.

4

Inflight Exorcism

Bangkok-bound flight, just a handful of passengers, a lot of action, too much initiative. A female passenger asks me to move to a different row, then for a glass of champagne, a G&T, a Bloody Mary... one thing leads to another and an hour later we find her striding a passenger! Carousel time!

Some hypo-imaginative passengers enquire, "What are they doing?"

Not the right time to go into details. I just say that's how they've fallen asleep. We must act promptly.

Once informed about the close encounter, the captain orders their separation. In line with current legislation, we must read out loud a warning letter, as per protocol. Besides informing them about the possible consequences, we also need witnesses.

We get closer.

"In the name of the law, we would like to inform you that your lewd and lascivious behaviour onboard this UK-registered aircraft might lead to arrest and criminal conviction. Therefore, we demand you stop immediately."

The exorcism works at once. The riding stops and the Valkyrie feigns on the spot while he asks for medical assistance. Let's pretend we buy into it. We would never deny a bottle of oxygen to anyone. The Amazon comes around in the blink of an eye and complains about some kind of pain... Possibly due to excessive rotation. But above all, the spinning session is over, and passengers can go back to the usual flying tedium. The girl will recover, the protocol has been followed, and, most importantly, the Crown is safe!

5

No Flowers, Just a Charitable Contribution

"This way, Mr Fassbender." Yes, none other than Michael Fassbender, the silver screen star. I take him to First Class and ask him to sit down in 1A, in the midst of curious glimpses of nearby passengers.

"Could I have my pyjamas, please, so I won't have to disturb you later?"

"Of course, my colleague will also show you where your duvet is in case you want to sleep after take-off, Mr Fassbender…"

"You can call me Michael. I can read 'Franco' on your name badge and it's not fair, I can't call you by your surname!"

This Fassbender is a charming gentleman, I wish all celebrities were just as nice!

Three hours later.

Mr Fassbender - although I am sure he wouldn't mind if I referred to him as Michael - sleeps like a baby under his soft duvet. But the atmosphere all around him is electrical.

"Is it true that Mr Fassbender is on board?"

"Yes, he is in First Class and fast asleep."

"But I adore him, I have always loved him; could I take a wee photo with him?"

"No, he is having a rest now, he doesn't want to be disturbed. And he's wearing his pyjamas by the way."

She swallows.

"I beg you, please let me have a peek from a distance. Just a little peep and then I'll go back to my seat. I mean, have you seen him in *Shame*? Is it… all real?"

"What?"

"Well, it wasn't a camera trick, was it?"

"Listen, I don't know, we are not allowed to look at the groin area, I just check boarding cards and that's about it!"

"Aw! He's so handsome!"

"But how can you tell if he's sleeping with his head tucked under the covers?"

"I can tell by the way he's sleeping… I can see him. And what's that? Can I borrow a flower from that bouquet in the toilet?" she asks pointing at something behind me.

"What for?"

"Can I lay one on his duvet whilst he's asleep? I will tiptoe next to his chair like a kitten, drop the rose and then I'll disappear; nobody will ever know, I swear to God."

"Absolutely not! In First Class everything is dark, private, solemn, and deadly as it is, if you come and lay a flower on sleeping Fassbender's duvet, it becomes a morgue. No way! Enough, please return to your seat; you've already had a brief eye encounter with him, does it not suffice?"

I can't be too hard for too long. I give in to her begging eyes.

"Just one attempt. You can't cross that line."

She presses the ground with her left foot before she starts to run and stops right at the foul line consigning the revolving rose to the air. It's a leap of faith. She won't have a second chance. She follows the flower with her eye and all the love she's got in her.

The flight of hope.

Here rests Michael Fassbender with a rose on his chest.

I categorically forbid her to rejoice aloud. I have a good mind to gag her, but she covers her mouth with her hand and jumps with joy instead.

"One last thing. Should he ask who left it when he wakes up, could you give him this?"

"Yes, of course, but now please go back to your seat."

"Thank you so much from the bottom of my aching heart."

I immediately tear up her business card, this has gone far enough. So dark! So quiet! And now even a rose, that's all I need to fall asleep myself.

What ever happened to charitable contributions?

6

Dirty Laundry and *Pasta & Fazul*

"In your own time… If I wait for you, I will get to New York in a fortnight! What was the point in explaining everything to the lady in the lounge, you tell me!"

"Ma'am, what happened?"

"Darling, choose your words more carefully! What did NOT happen!"

There we go! We haven't even taken off yet and I have already forgotten that, regardless of what happens, it is always my fault. I wonder what the benefits of wearing a uniform are. They say that many women still find themselves drawn to a man in uniform… in this case I am failing miserably!

"Anyway, can I leave my dirty laundry here in this bag?" she says while starting to rummage in her wheelie bag, oblivious of the long queue of passengers behind her who, for some strange reason, would like to get on board. Are they here because they want to fly by any chance?

"Ma'am, if you can't find something, would you mind stepping aside so that we can let other passengers on?"

"We are really speaking two different languages, aren't we? What do you mean if I can't find something? I might be ancient, narcoleptic and a New Yorker but…"

The latter condition is the one that worries me the most…

"It will take me no time to find my dirty underwear, I know where I put it, and since I'm not blind, I can see very well that you have a dirty laundry bag. What's the problem? Don't tell me that on a seven-hour flight you can't wash it for me!"

"Sorry ma'am but the bag that you see on the jetty is just our onboard First Class laundry from the previous flight, it stays here in London."

"Well, how many people and things are you planning to leave behind today? An old narcoleptic lady who should have left on the morning flight is forced to get home on the evening service… and now you don't want to wash my laundry? What's the point of flying First Class?"

To lose touch with reality. It should be abolished!

Anyhow, we manage to finish boarding and close the door; Sleepy is comfortably seated and will get her laundry washed in Manhattan. Deep breath, Ellis Island here we come…

Dinnertime in Business Class.

"Granny, I don't want anything to eat because… you are a silly cow!"

"Don't call me that, you are not at home! Be a good girl. Tell Franco what you want for dinner."

"No, I am not going to tell him anything; they always have the usual crap food! You know what I like, you tell him!"

"Young lady, watch your language!"

Ellis Island is getting closer, I can nearly make out the liberty crown that will set me free.

"I know that you want pasta & fazul. Franco, you are Italian, aren't you? If you want, he can make pasta & fazul for you!"

We forgive you for having distorted most names of our dishes; but how can I possibly make pasta & fazul, how you call it, at 42,000 feet over the Atlantic? As if we were not busy enough with washing Sleepy's underwear in First Class!

"Yesss, Granny! I want pasta & fazul!!!"

What happened to the American girls of our dreams who live on popcorns and marshmallows?

I have a brilliant idea. Something that will fit the bill!

"OK, let me finish the service and then I will make you *pasta & fazul!*"

"Granny, granny, is Franco really going to make me pasta & fazul???"

I wrap up the service in the cabin as quickly as possible and I immediately talk to my colleague. Any hostess worth her name has a bag or a tub of freeze-dried soup, usually Weight Watchers', in her wheelie bag!

"Yes, Franco, you can use it, it's been there for donkey's years. It's in my handbag in the wardrobe, I think it's macaroni. But what's *fazul*?"

"Don't worry, I will tell you later. Thank you very much!"

I get the makeshift soup from my colleague's bag, I add a little bit of hot water, et voilà, dried macaroni comes back to life under my very eyes. I still have to solve the *fazul* problem. We have a spare Asian meal… Eureka! I will pass lentils off as beans!

"Granny, this pasta & fazul is DIVINE, yours is awful!!! Get his recipe!"

"If you finish it up, I will give you a dollar."

"Just ONE dollar?"

"Franco, could you please…"

Sorry, I need to go to Fist Class and wake Sleepy up, very soon we will be landing, I don't want her to carry on sleeping and end up going back to London! I must also remember to write to the airline with this brilliant new idea: *Wash&Dry as You Fly®*!

7

Transiting Crew

If it ain't Boeing, I ain't going.

But no, my dear! From today, you have been thrown in at the deep end of the Airbus 380; so, gone are the days of 'doors to automatic' or 'doors to manual and cross check'. From now on, you will 'arm' and 'disarm' slides and will 'cross-dress' (sorry, cross-check) with your colleague on the opposite door. But where's the shuttle to move from one aisle to the next? No laugh, because there certainly is a lift, but we old school prefer staircases; we wouldn't like to get stuck on an aircraft elevator, engineers might take forever.

"You're so lucky," our instructor says, "some charter airline A380s have a capacity of up to 879 passengers. Here, only 469."

Only? For me, though, who up until yesterday used to fly on my beloved Boeing 767 - the Skoda of the Skies, which with one can of kerosene would go there and back from the Bahamas as smooth as silk -, for me that for over twenty years have been flying on this 'retrieving aircraft', the A380 just does not do it. Why did they have to retire it? I have half a mind to go to the Arizona desert, in the aircraft cemetery, to take them all back. Yes, when they are deemed unfit to fly, they are sent to the driest place on Earth, a sort of avionic Paradise, to be mothballed. Apparently, there, they don't rust; but has it ever occurred to anyone to write on the dusty fuselage 'AGEISM SUCKS'? Yes, I think some of them would quite happily still take to the skies. It's all Airbus' fault!

"So, did you really fly on the 767?" a new entrant asks me at the cabin crew training centre during our coffee break.

Now, I'm going to tell him/her that I flew on the Concorde, just to see how he/she reacts. One good thing about this airline is that nobody gets checked under the tail. Easy for them, though, they have your documents. But how am I supposed to address this chimera with legs that go on for days, a baritone voice, a hint of a bump in the groin area, a dark stubble, and a doe-eyed gaze?

"My name is Giada and I am here on a cabin crew new-entrant course and I really wanted to know what it was like flying on the 767, 'cause I can only imagine that you didn't have a chance to fly on the 737, right?"

"No, I started on the Eagle 1, my trainer was shapeshifting Maya and one year later I got promoted onto the Voyager."

This Giada is really getting on my ailerons, I hope it's just a transitional phase! The hard truth, though, is that I really flew on every single aircraft that she mentioned, and here I am for yet another conversion!

The torture continues.

"So, I imagine you all applied for the A380 conversion course, did you not?"

You're really missing the point. I, Homo Boeing, You, Airbus!

"And now for the door opening and closing procedures. Guys, please, remember that pressure gauge? You don't want to fly another child into a dispatcher's arms, do you?"

As if all the other checks weren't enough, now I also have to remember to look for a flashing light before opening the door, otherwise a child might end up splattered on the tarmac.

"And also, during an evacuation, you must use the right commands, otherwise I will have to fail you. Now, we'll show you a video of a simulation; you must be like a Rottweiler, you have 80 seconds to evacuate the whole aircraft. Do like the crew member on the video. Agreed? We chose an airline at random."

"Raus, Raussssssss!" the hydrophobic Teutonic crew member shouts while first pushing passengers down one aisle and then chasing them up the other... almost biting them at their heels. "Ich habe rauch gesaaaaaaaaaaacht!"

"See? That's the way you should do it. It does not matter if she's German! That's the way it should be done. You are not doing a make-up course. Otherwise, we would have shown you an Air France video."

This instructor is sooo funny.

"Are you ready, Franco?"

"Ready as I'll ever be."

"Ditching. You are at Door 5 left on the main deck. What do you shout to passengers?

Hang on a minute, has this aircraft got two decks? Can't believe it.

"Jump, jump, form two lines!"

"Noooo! Passengers at door 5, in the event of a ditching, must run! The command is 'Run, run', because the slide is tilted slightly upwards. And at Door 1 and 2 in a land evacuation, what would you shout to passengers? Do you remember Helga on the video?"

Well, I remember her face very well, but then she spoke German and I don't think she uttered much more than 'Raus', but I'll give it a go, with Airbus it's always a wild guess, anyway.

"Stay on your feet and keep moving!"

"Noooo! That's at Door 3 because the slide is flat!"

But, in an emergency, how do you get someone to run, others to waddle off and still others to pretend they are on a theme park's inflatables?

Oh, my beloved 767, I miss you so much!

Somebody come up with a plus,

For working on an Airbus!

8

The Chain of Love

"Champagne, orange juice, water?"

No sign of life.

Second attempt.

"Champagne, orange juice, water?"

Uncomfortably seated in 12B in Business, Mr Gomez looks at me as if he saw a ghost and repeatedly crosses himself, each time using a different technique: from left to right, from right to left, blowing kisses to the air, crossing himself on the forehead... a jumble of styles probably verging on heresy!

"I'm still missing three!"

Uhm, interesting. I hope Mr Gomez will expand on that; meanwhile I try to gather my thoughts... Three what, exactly? Three trading cards to complete his collection... three screws not loose but missing in his brain...Enough, I can't work it out.

"Three what, Mr Gomez?"

"I'm still missing three messages from my chain of love; we are all seeing the same therapist. There are ten of us and when faced with difficult situations, we send each other supporting messages to help us through!"

"I see... but what's difficult at the moment?"

"Are you kidding me? Take-off scores 5 in our group's internal code; if you think that a head-on collision scores 6, then you get the picture! If I don't receive those three messages, and they knew I was flying today, honest to God, I won't be able to make it! Just hold on, I will call my therapist and ask him whether I can drink champagne before orange juice, this is what you wanted to know, isn't it?"

"Yes, but it doesn't really matter; would you care for a glass of water, Mr Gomez?"

Too late, he is already on the phone.

Just when you think you've seen it all, here comes the drink therapist!

"So, he's telling me that I'd better mix them; give me another glass, please. If I do as he says everything will be just fine (*What kind of therapy is this!*). He's also telling me that, although he's religious, he's not a church-going person, so he doesn't know if I crossed myself the right way. I think from left to right is how you are supposed to do it, but I am not dead sure about it! Dead! My goodness! Why am I using this kind of words? Franco, you must be a catholic as well, could you help me, please?"

What am I going to say now? I catch a glimpse of the rosary lying on the tray table and I come up with a makeshift solution.

"Mr Gomez, the way you cross yourself doesn't really matter. When in doubt, you just pray the rosary anticlockwise and everything will be fine. That's what I do, and it works all the time. It's like asking for forgiveness, Mr Gomez."

"I knew you were a good catholic boy. I'm still missing two messages; I will pray the rosary as you said, when I get to the Mysteries, will you help me, though?"

"Of course! Now I need to close the door, check the cabin for take-off and sit down. Let me know when you get to the Joyful Mysteries, but in the meantime, pray the rosary from left to right."

Oh, Saint Joseph of Cupertino, "The Flying Friar", help us!

9

Sometimes They Come back

Tonight, between a Boston and a Philadelphia, we are back to our quaint little village. Here we are, in our local Chinese takeaway restaurant for something to enjoy in the peace of our cottage with our pussy cat.

"Franco, is that you?" asks a guy who has just come in.

Yes, that's my name… I think… but I'm so jet lagged that I might be hearing voices. But more importantly, who are YOU?

"My favourite steward! Last week, you were on my flight to Cairo, do you remember?"

On such occasions, I feel like substitute teachers; they go from school to school, never recognize any pupils while students always remember them!

"How come? We even stayed at the same hotel in Cairo. Do you remember we went for a swim together? Seriously, you don't recognize me?"

I spend half my life in a trance, imagine if I can remember passengers; but he insists and is getting louder and louder, so much so that in the Chinese takeaway no one is interested in food anymore. The owner puts the fryer on hold. Little villages feed on gossip!

"Do you remember I was sitting by the window? You only had tagliatelle left and I told you I couldn't have it because it makes me fart."

Flatulence triggers my memory.

"Oh yes, it's all coming back to me now! You got so stroppy that I had to go to Business Class to get some beef otherwise you wouldn't stop moaning."

"Yes, it works every time, even with Emirates! When I start talking about farting, they bring me whatever I want, even from First Class sometimes!"

"Really?" enquires the curious Chinese guy behind the counter while taking mental notes. He's so engrossed in the conversation that he's stopped answering the phone.

"What an amazing coincidence! You also live in Calne-of-All-Places. So, I can come to yours to have a bite together, you little bugger!"

Nice… and very direct…Nice terms of endearment!

"Look, I'll go and get my dog, I'll take him for a shite, have a pint down the local and then come straight to your place. Is that ok with you?"

If I came to a takeaway, I might want to enjoy my food in the peace of my own home, don't you think? Plus, I need an early night. Tomorrow I'll be off to Philly.

The Chinese chap looks in disbelief, he doesn't understand: farts, pasta, Italians in Wiltshire, pooing dogs… I think he'd rather shut up shop and call it a day.

Mr Gassy leaves, promising to come back asap.

"But was he really in Business Class?" ask the Chinese guy and another customer holding his takeaway bag but with no intention to leave before getting an answer.

"No, in the depths of Economy!"

"I was gonna say!"

"Yes, but he scoffed the Business Class beef alright, didn't he?" adds the Chinese fellow.

"By any chance, can you spare a plastic bag? He had a massive dump in the church alley, and I ain't got any bags on me," says the former passenger opening the door with his dog behind him on a leash. Then he turns to me and says, "Franco wait for me, I'll be back in 10 minutes max!"

Some passengers really stand out for their finesse.

But wouldn't it be better if he went home and washed his hands… and mouth, perhaps?

10

Aquagym

"Excuse me, I am a gynaecologist!"

"I think he might have tendinitis; I don't know whether this is your field…"

"I know, but had I told you that I was a doctor, you would have asked me 'doctor of medicine?' So, to save time, I state my specialisation straight away. It's my duty, anyway. Thinking about it, I am hardly ever off duty. It's been years since I last savoured a film at the cinema, a show at a theatre and often I have to cut short my holidays as well. Oftentimes I do wonder why I took that Hippocratic oath all those years ago…"

"I think even a midwife would do at this stage, the pain at my Achilles tendon is excruciating! Ouch! I need a painkiller!" shouts the passenger who is now in the position of a beetle in metamorphosis, belly up with his black Lycra runner outfit.

For now, we're leaving him in the Kafkaesque position; he had it coming and we take a step back.

"Now I'm going to ask you something that might sound peculiar to you," tells me the passenger sitting at 17A, after pressing the call bell.

"Yes, madam, how can I help you?"

"Could you bring me a bottle of water?"

"Of course, straight away."

"Yes, speed is essential... I know it will seem bizarre to you, but I am following the quick water diet. In a while, Dr Kimberly will publish his book about it."

And then people wonder why the publishing industry is not doing well.

"In short, I have to drink three glasses of water, or even four, as quickly as I possibly can, and even the doctor recommends doing it with a trusted friend who's supposed to fill your glass... At the beginning, it might even seem an amusing experience, but the reality is that you are cheating your system. The water creates a vortex, in other words, the pit of the stomach opens up and before it shuts again you must fill it up with water. Zero calories, job done! Thus, the stomach won't ask you for anything else for hours. It's either this or lap band surgery. I'm used to this by now, sometimes though I find it hard to drink it quickly enough, but I'm getting better by the minute. Since you're such a sweetheart, would you like to play with me a little?"

Quite a responsibility! If I fail, the lady will go under the knife.

"Alright, madam, If I got you right, I must fill your glass up with water as soon as I see it empty, right?"

"Yes, but straight away, remember! Otherwise, the pit closes up. Anyway, it's all written down in the book."

As if I had time to read it.

Ready, steady, go.

I fill up the glass. The spectacled lady takes a deep breath and brings the tumbler to her lips.

First vision.

In front of me there's a cleft-palate goldfish that has been trapped in a glass bowl for the past twenty years. I have a feeling it is dangerously approaching my face. Its eyes are about to pop out, it is demanding the dry food that somebody has forgotten to give it for at least fifteen days.

"More!"

I pour the second glass. She lifts the tumbler and takes it to her mouth.

Second vision.

I am trapped in a maze surrounded by distorting mirrors and I am being chased by a pair of piranha jaws in search of food but, unfortunately, they only find water. A Ferris wheel of images all around me: pit of the stomach about to close up, rivers of water streaming down the pylorus and the looming threat of stomach stapling.

"Last one!"

Third vision.

The Church will not accept unfair competition with Fatima.

I move away from the gasping lady who's hungry for air and meanwhile dries up her tears for the exertion.

"Thanks! Did I make funny faces?" she asks me with a smile.

"I'll explain later," I reply to her trying to disconnect from my Neuro-visions.

What ever happened to the man with tendinitis?

"Has he fallen?"

"No, perhaps, he overdid it."

"Yes!" replies the woman next door. "He hasn't stopped going up and down the whole aircraft with that bloody pedometer, but this is no sports field!"

"I have diabetes!" protests the beetle on the floor.

"We are going to give you a pain killer and then when we land in Chicago the paramedics will come on board with a wheelchair. Now you must take it easy, you'll get off first, rest assured."

"In a wheelchair? But don't they have crutches?"

"Just a precaution."

Chicago.

The paramedics come on board and wheel the creepy crawly off the plane.

"I'm not crippled! I was training for the Brisk Walking Championship inside the Mall on the Magnificent Mile. I'm not even diabetic. I'm just pre!" he exclaims to passengers while they inexorably push him towards the exit.

In my next life, I want to be Dr Kimberly. Water for everybody. Sparkling on a Sunday.

11

Lost in Translation

In the galley, bending over my bar trolley, I'm trying to take out a London Pride for a passenger who, determined to give some relief to his unquenchable thirst, has been jingling the call bell for quite a while.

"I am beside myself! Over the moon!" shouts an American lady slamming the toilet door behind her. "Finally, my dream has come true," she continues.

Since she's just come out of the loo, I can't quite understand what sort of dream she might have fulfilled, but in the meantime let me take a beer to that gentleman, I'll think about it on my way.

I come back to the galley.

"I've bought a house in Capri!" she exclaims. "After twenty long years thinking and dreaming of it, I managed to do it!" the lady, and no-one else, rejoices. "No big deal, Franco. A far cry from a Roman villa! A one-bedroom apartment, but with a view over the sea to die for!" she explains ecstatically. "I don't speak Italian, but the locals call me 'la newyorkese' (the she-New Yorker), they just adore me. A few things still puzzle me, though. Last time I went back there, I found the windows wide open; they had already told me something down in the marina. They always say I don't understand and that I have to leave my door key with them or leave the door open. A house shouldn't be left closed for so many months, it just dies from the inside, of dampness, so they forced themselves in, to let some fresh air into the house. And they also say that nobody locks their house doors in Capri, only Americans do. I am not used to so much familiarity, would you trust them, Franco?"

"Look, from Bolzano downwards I would think twice before trusting anybody, but each to their own, perhaps they've taken quite a shine on you."

"And I like it when they talk to me in Italian, I want to learn your beautiful language so that I can chat with everyone and sing opera under the shower. Last week I went down to the beach and a few local boys were chit-chatting; as I was unfolding my beach towel, they said, 'Ah, la newyorkese, che bella falsa magra!' which literally translated means 'Ah, the she-New Yorker, what a lovely false slim lady!' I felt like Sophia Loren by the way they were staring at me!!! Well, I know I don't really understand all the hidden layers of meaning contained in such a beautiful expression, but they said it while eyeing me up, it was so thrilling! Could you please expand on this concept which, I understand, if literally translated, loses its shine a bit?"

"Yes, in Italy, it's quite a common expression. What they meant is that you have a strong aesthetic sense, and your choice of bikini was excellent... that's all."

Frankly, never in my life had I thought that one day I would have to explain the all-Italian concept of 'false slim'. All things considered, I handled it rather well.

"Really?" she asks in awe. "Actually, since I've been living in Italy, my fashion sense has skyrocketed and I am extremely pleased that somebody has noticed that, especially the locals; I want to become an honorary Capri citizen, the false slim she-New Yorker of the whole island of Capri!"

And she lived falsely slim ever after on the enchanted island of Capri.

12

WHO

Going to work in the wake of WHO's historic announcement seriously damages the physical, but primarily mental health … of us cabin crew.

"Do you mind counting the meals while I try to sort out the flush in Toilet M?" asks my colleague before they release the beasts at the gate. "Hurry up, they will be here soon; we also have ten wheelchairs and a blind or deaf, I can't remember exactly."

Sure, one of those generic disabilities not worth memorising… but that makes a world of difference to them!

I open the oven. I am overwhelmed by the unusual stench of an abandoned canary cage that fixes my hair for the rest of the flight! A massacre of Guinea Fowl Cacciatora and just TWO British Beef for Economy Plus. I've never seen such an abundance of avifauna on a plane before!

"But how have all these guinea fowls managed to fly into the oven? Never seen them before!" I say to my colleague while he is still busy trying to fix the toilet before the imminent boarding.

"Guinea what? Foul, as in F-O-U-L? It's a bird, isn't it?"

"I know the smell is FOUL, but it's F-O-W-L, by the way. And yes, it is a bird, it's like a... chicken."

"Never been good at spelling. Anyway, chickens don't make a real nest, do they? But guinea FOWLS do make a nest and fly, don't they? I think I know what they are."

I am not sure he has understood; after all, guinea fowl has been out of fashion for years, it hasn't been on any menu for decades. I don't understand what the occasion for today's sacrifice might be.

"I suspect that after WHO's announcement, they are digging out poultry that nobody would ever eat in normal circumstances. But who are we going to foist it upon?"

To be honest, I also thought that guinea fowl belonged to an extinct food category, but how could they come up with it so quickly? Where did they get it from? For how long has it been in a deep freezer waiting to fly back with a vengeance after the announcement? WHO knows?!

"Fuck WHO!" concludes John, my colleague. "Now Brussels is telling us what to eat! I can't stand EU laws!"

"WHO is actually a global organisation having nothing to do with the EU."

"It doesn't matter; it's a foreign organisation alright. In England, we are used to eating cows; before you know it, they'll impose budgies on us!"

Let's hope guinea fowl is not met with the same disdain by passengers otherwise we will be in big trouble.

"Would you care for guinea fowl cacciatora or British beef, ma'am?"

"I chose as soon as I read the menu," answers the lady sitting in 30H in Economy Plus, her eyes brimming with nostalgia. "Give me guinea fowl cacciatora, and I will also tell you why you made my day, but not now, later!"

Thank you, ma'am; I'm all a-tither!

"Is the beef really... red today?" asks the passenger in the next row.

I glare at him, roll my eyes *The Exorcist* style, it might just do the trick.

"To be on the safe side, I'll go for guinea fowl, I'm very health conscious!"

Guinea fowl might become prescribable in the blink of an eye!

I manage to get to the back of Economy almost unscathed; guinea fowl has been welcomed with open jaws, meanwhile I'm told they need a pair of helping hands in Business. I get there *in media res* when the fight has already broken off.

"I WANT BEEF! I don't even know what guinea fowl is! Plus, I'm ornithophobic, I'm scared of birds, dead or alive. It's not a bird, is it?"

"Sir," tries to explain Zoe, "after yesterday's WHO announcement, maybe for today they tried something more..."

"More what?" presses her the passenger increasingly upset. "I don't give a damn! You must have some sort of beef on a British airline! I'm not choosy, I eat any animal, as long as it has four legs! In Colorado we aren't picky, I would even eat a coyote if you had it... or an armadillo, but a plucked bird? No way! And what's this business with WHO announcement? So, what are you serving in First Class today? Flamingo, by any chance? I mean, since it has pink flesh... Anyway, why don't *you* have a bit of cock yourself?"

Help! We urgently need to find some kind of quadruped otherwise we will have to divert...

Ding, ding

I answer the call bell in Business Class.

"I'd like some paracetamol, but I had guinea fowl. Do you know if it can interfere with it?"

Till this morning, I really liked guinea fowls; they are so elegant, but can I hate WHO just a little for creating all these problems? How the hell would I know?!

"Just let me check ma'am, I'll read the patient package insert and see if it mentions anything," I answer professionally. I consult with Poker-face Mario who solves the problem in a flash. "Ma'am, we got in touch with WHO via radio; you can take two tablets, you'll be absolutely fine."

What about if it were pigeon? Would Mario have an answer for that as well? I will think about it when the problem arises. Thank God for Mario!

I sneak off to Economy where guinea fowl has been a huge success, so much so that... do you remember the lady in Economy Plus? Visibly moved, she thanks me profusely and she even asks for a comment card. When she gives it back to me, I can't resist, I must have a peak before handing it in.

I would like to thank you for the delicious 'Guinea Fowl Cacciatora'! It took me back to my childhood, a wonderful trip down sweet memory lane. As a little girl, I used to visit my nana in the countryside. She had many animals: pigs, chickens, chicks etc. but my favourite were guinea fowls. I spent hours playing with them, they would jump on my lap, I would stroke them. Ah, those amazing black and white specks! Then I remember my granny catching them, she caressed their necks and in two seconds flat they would stop moving. She would tell me that they were asleep and would stay with us for dinner but that soon afterwards they would fly to Guinea Heaven where they would have fun with the others, showing off, singing, and dancing. When I grew up, I understood that she wanted to teach me not to feel guilty for eating them; therefore, today it was a very emotional and beautiful occasion for me.

Sorry to share this intimate story with you… but I think it was an amazing gesture on your part. Long live Guinea Fowls and Long Live the Queen! A very satisfied customer.

An ode to cognitive dissociation.

I reseal the comment card. I go and check in First Class. That passenger in Business just piqued my curiosity… if there is chicken in Economy, guinea fowl in Economy Plus… Heaven forbid, in First Class they might really serve flamingo!

Enough! PETA must have a word with WHO!

13

Blinding Documentaries

"Just to recap. You wake up, you can't open your hand, and you are as white as a sheet. Don't worry I'll give you some oxygen and you'll be fine."

I put the brake on and go to Business Class to fetch the first cure-all oxygen bottle I can lay my hands on. While I'm there, a passenger asks me, "The guy over there has had his face glued to that video for a good fifteen minutes; do you think he is alright?" And her partner confirms, "Yes, I've noticed it as well, I think he has freeze-framed it."

I walk up to the old chap who, while snoring, is dribbling on his teacup on the table.

"Is he asleep now?" asks his wife sitting next to him.

"Completely gone, ma'am."

"If he is dribbling, it means he is fast asleep. You can turn it off."

I approach the screen and notice that he has freeze-framed the movie on a curvy babe with her back so overarched that it might break anytime... *He is (was) watching, 'Body Language' on Discovery Channel...interesting.*

I go back to my 'numbed' lady and suspect she might have been watching Discovery Channel as well. I put her on oxygen and after a couple of minutes she makes a full recovery. She glances at me as if I were the best thing since sliced bread, turns round, and carries on with the documentary.

Meanwhile, in Business Class on the upper deck, another passenger is on oxygen. I don't want to know what he was watching; we are getting ready for landing.

"Cabin crew, doors to manual and cross-check."

Engines off, chocks on. The captain speaks over the PA. "Ladies and gentlemen, we would kindly ask you to remain seated with your seatbelts fastened. A passenger on our upper-deck cabin has been taken ill, we are just waiting for the paramedics to board the aircraft. I will let you know when you can disembark. Thank you for your cooperation."

My colleague on the other aisle, still sitting on her jump seat, is trying to tell me something, half speaking and half gesticulating, but I get the gist... "Do you know what happened?"

"No, I don't. Tell me."

"On landing, the guy upstairs lost his sight. Completely blind! He can't tell day from night. He realised it when he noticed he couldn't see the documentary anymore and called our colleague!"

True, some landings can be pretty traumatic for your retina, but here the thread seems to be that Mama Jama on Discovery Channel... I wonder what he was doing with his hands to go suddenly blind.

Maybe he skipped a few Sunday school lessons.

14

Moving and Removing 39 K

"Move 39 K to 17 K," whispers out of breath the cabin manager at the boarding door. I was just looking for a pack of nuts to munch on in the peace and quiet of Economy.

"Who?" I ask, but words fail me.

"Hurry up! I'll explain everything later, Franco."

It sounds like an order.

I get up to Miss Go-Lucky; she is surprised, suspicious, and gives me a questioning look. I must not attract any attention; moreover, I haven't got any explanation to offer, so I have to be discreet.

"Ma'am, I think there was a mistake with your boarding card. Just follow me, please."

The other passengers give us envious, dirty looks.

As soon as she sees me turning left, she can't believe her eyes, and in no time, she manages to collect all her belongings and follows me wagging her tail like a poodle on a catwalk.

I pass by my colleague at Door 3 who tries to gather intel. I whisper to him, "Liam, do you know who this lady I'm taking up to Business is?"

"No idea, but she's a knockout! Hot stuff, mate!" he says gobsmacked, completely oblivious of the fact that cutie-pie can hear everything.

Well, since I'm none the wiser, I take the bombshell to 17 K and help her put her luggage away. She is as bewildered as I am. She can't believe her luck and sits immediately down on her newly inherited throne.

Another colleague comes round with some welcome drinks, the upgraded 'Hottie', as Liam would call her, feels immediately at home and gets into character.

"For me, a Buck's Fizz, please!"

I'm about to turn tail when I see the cabin manager waving his arms at me from the galley; he looks like an air traffic controller, but I'm not familiar with those signs, so I go up to him.

"Take her back to Economy!" he orders, "There's been a mistake, we are chock-a-block!"

What's going on? How can I break the terrible news to Hottie-Got-Lucky? I know that five minutes in Business are better than nothing, but you can't play with people's feelings and emotions like this.

"Don't worry, I'll delete everything if you want," she reassures me gratefully.

Maybe she has noticed the embarrassed look on my face. She's so terrified to have to go back to Economy that she deletes all her selfies under my very eyes. The only proof of her 5 minutes of stardom, all gone.

"No problem," she tells me drinking up the last drop of her Buck's Fizz while trying to gather her whole kit and caboodle. "Brief but utterly intense, I'd say. That really made my day. I don't need any explanation. There's nothing to understand, these things do happen."

In the meantime, here comes a lady wearing a mink fur coat down to her ankles, a pair of black leggings, humungous sunglasses, and a pair of Richard-the-Lionheart boots. She sits down on the seat recently vacated by the shuttle girl.

"Just one molecule, do you understand?"

Half utterances are always extremely dangerous.

You've never seen me before in your life, our paths have just crossed for the first time on this plane and do you truly expect me to understand your enigmatic sentences?

I ask my colleague; he enlightens me on the lady's condition. Not only is she allergic to any kind of nuts, but even an atom (a neutrino?) could send her into anaphylactic shock. She could even pop her clogs!

The cabin manager checks the airline's protocol, so to cover our back we must make an announcement. Lucy volunteers to help.

"Ladies and Gentlemen, we would like to inform you that on today's flight we have a passenger with a severe PENIS allergy...bla...bla..bla.. thank you."

Half the plane bursts into laughter.

"Why are they laughing?" asks Lucy.

"Well, Lucy, instead of PEANUTS you've just said PENIS! What's in your mind?! By the look of it, the lady might be allergic to peanuts, but I'm not so sure she's intolerant to...ah ah ah..." comments the cabin manager.

"Please tell me this is not true!!!" grunts embarrassed Lucy.

She grabs the interphone.

"PEANUTS allergy, sorry!"

The other half of the plane who didn't laugh with the first announcement now bursts into laughter too.

"Franco, 34K's legs, do they fit under the seat?" asks me the cabin manager. "I'm so upset that I couldn't keep her in Business! But you never know, we could show a peanut to 17 K to send her into anaphylactic shock and free her seat!"

15

The Umbrellaed, the Framed and the Slitted

"Fifteen, Francisco!" shouts from underneath her head-to-toe umbrella the Lady Caliph pointing her ringed finger and vanishing in First Class.

The problem with working in Business on the 777 is that the galley dangerously borders with First Class, so you are neither here nor there, poised between two universes. Hard as you try not to fall into the abyss, in practice you end up working everywhere. The worst of both worlds!

"Excuse me, Mina, what should I do, according to her?" I ask my Bahraini colleague.

He enquires with the emir's wife on the right-hand side. Yes, today our First Class is split in two: one emir on the left with wives and children on tow and another emir on the right with just as many wives and offspring. Let the battle of the oil fields begin!

"She wants to buy fifteen perfumes of your choice from the duty-free bar."

Sometimes a stab in a non-vital body part, such as your behind for instance, is less painful. Will I ever be able to please someone who addresses me with the wrong name even though she's just read it on my name badge? Does she want men's or ladies' fragrances, anyway?

"Eau de Parfum!" she demands drawing the First Class curtain to separate herself from the far too crowded Business Class.

Order received.

I set up the rosé champagne glasses for Business passengers. The emirs' children keep on trotting from one aisle to the next in an endless loop, they have already spilled two glasses of wine on a single seat.

"Franco, they've brought down a suitcase full of toys and they scattered them all over First, they seem to be out of control. Before take-off, do you mind giving us a hand to put them back into the suitcase? They can't stop chasing each other, they are running around like headless chickens!"

Enough! Time has come for Abu Said to enter the scene.

I grab the champagne ice bucket, magically transformed into my tambourine, and I become an Arab bard.

"And thus, from far away came Abu Said…"

On hearing that name, the children suddenly stop. But then it is a bit like playing the cymbals in an orchestra. You draw attention to yourself and now what is Abu Said going to do?

And Abu Said,

Who saw the rough sea…

Bom, bom, bom, bom,

I recite drumming my fingers on the plastic container.

My colleague on the other aisle is looking at me in a state of shock and to be honest I, myself, don't know where all this is going.

"The children want to know whether you are Egyptian and if you know all the adventures of Abu Said," Mina translates for me.

So, it really works then; I can carry on saying whatever I want about Abu Said in my own mother tongue.

"Yes, tell them I know them all, but I can sing them in an old Egyptian dialect, and they need to understand from my gestures, but they MUST sit down."

"Ok, but they want you to finish the first verse, otherwise they won't sit down for take-off."

Chose to come through the desert

On his red horse in his blue shirt…

Bom, bom, bom

The children are sitting down at last. We can leave now.

Bar service.

"But is she my mum?" asks me a child lying down on the Business Class seat with his headsets on and pointing at the black bundle next to him.

"Are you being serious?"

"Yes, can't you see that I'm watching a movie? I didn't notice when she lay down, can you please tell me if it's her?"

The Filipino nanny barges in and points at the foot of his alleged mother. The boy lifts the veil up from the woman's foot and punches her on the talon with a noticeable thickening of the skin. His mother is numb, she does not react. But he is sure now and crashes down on her.

"Mum, I'm hungry and thirsty, all at the same time!"

"Mashallah!" shouts his mother with her hands to the sky. "Give him a Kofta Kebab and a Coke, but take him off me, please!"

I carry on, sometimes it gets better.

"Franco, you must tell the cabin manager to come down the back immediately, we have a problem with the slitted."

I find myself more at ease with the umbrellaed and the framed; the slitted, kind of embarrass me, they stare at me with those eyes, they look like bumper cars… they make me go off road, that's it.

"What's up?" asks the cabin manager noticing a heap of stuff on the floor.

"They are having fun," answers their mother. "They are building a city with food leftovers, they're not harming anybody; if I don't let them do it, they are going to break her arm like they did last time," she warns pointing at the Asian nanny.

No, a diversion for a fractured nanny must be avoided at all costs! And where would that be? It's a sea of barren sand down there.

"Have you got a candied cherry or something red to put on top of the rice mountain? I am sure they'd be thrilled with that and they might even stop," says the Arabic woman with a broken voice, as if her husband's oil rig had just run dry.

Believe you me, we need to carry on supporting renewable energy, there's no alternative!

16

Perfume and Movement

"There's only 8 of us in the world with this disorder. It's called hyperosmia," she says while I'm accompanying her to 2A.

Since we are a very exclusive airline, only very special people fly with us. It sounds a little bit like insomnia, but I'm pretty sure that there are more than eight insomniacs on earth. What kind of rare disorder is Mrs Faye suffering from? I think we'd better lay all our cards on the table, just to be on the safe side. All I want to know is if a paracetamol or a little oxygen would do the trick, aerating your brain can only do you good.

"I have an increased olfactory acuity; I can smell odours that normally people can't; some of them can be fatal for me, though!"

Let's hope that on today's flight we don't have any passenger suffering from aerophagia. If so, what's the safety distance from the "hyperosmic"?

A legitimate question that is going through my mind, but I need to go back to the boarding door; I will come up with a spirometry strategy later, if needed.

"But don't worry, I'm always well-equipped when I travel."

The last customer is onboard, I close the door and take a copy of the passenger list to the cabin manager's office outside the flight deck, but my attention is drawn towards the not-so-well-identified object Mrs Faye is wearing on her nose. A plastic rhinoapparatus with two oversized filters, one on each side of her nose, that look like two magnified fly eyes. An amazing olfactory barrier from another planet!

"Don't give me that puzzled look! I know I look like an alien, but nothing can go through these," she says indicating the filters under her nostrils while trying to inhale.

My only consolation is that there are just seven other people in the world who must wear such monstrosity in public. Anyway, I don't work in First today, I was merely paying a courtesy visit.

I get the bar trolley ready in Business and start the service; today I also feel very talkative (Mrs Faye would call it loquaciousness), I really want to get to know my passengers.

"Mrs and Mr Pritchard, would you care for a drink?"

"We'd like to carry on with Buck's Fizz."

"What do you mean by 'carry on'? This is the first bar round. Are you already tipsy?" I banter with my best amicable tone perfected in over twenty years of f-lying.

"Darling, you should tell him that we have been travelling around the world for the past 150 days," his wife rebukes him.

"Yes, we are returning from a 150-day cruise around the world. You know, when you get to our age, I'm 80 and she's 81, travelling is a way of feeling alive. But more importantly, we both love 'movement', don't we Rose Sweetheart?" he says winking at her.

Two beautiful, perfectly tanned elderly people. I'm glad to be working in Business Class today and happy to see that things have changed. It's called evolution. I'm really pleased for them.

"In that case, I wish you a lot of turbulence today!"

"To be honest, I prefer rough… seas!" he says with a laugh.

Dead calm for two hours.

Coming back from my break, I pass by the Pritchards' flatbed seats. I squint, trying to focus, something is not right. I look at the pyjamas I'm holding in my hands; I'm not dreaming, I've just been for my break and I'm coming back into service so what I'm seeing should be real.

Dark cabin. Mr Pritchard standing in front of Mrs Pritchard who is lying down but propping herself up on her elbows. So far so good, but the problem is that he is… exposing himself!

There's nothing wrong…

In such embarrassing situations, you behave like real men do. You look at each other in the eyes and natter, but this happens when you are standing next to one another in front of a urinal; I can't find a common topic to discuss, plus, Mrs Pritchard, metaphorically speaking, has sneaked into the gents.

She looks at me quizzically, as if I were an engineer called to carry out some… emergency maintenance work. Mr Pritchard also stares at me proudly, satisfied with his morning glory. But his grandeur is very short-lived, much to Mrs Pritchard's disappointment. I pretend I haven't seen anything and head straight for the galley.

"Franco, thank God you're back!" the cabin manager says almost out of breath. "The Pritchards have been at it the whole time! I thought that at their age... but no! He's been on top of her as if there were no tomorrow. Impressive rabbity business! For how long can we pretend nothing is happening? In about an hour, we must start getting breakfast ready. Do *you* feel like talking to them?"

I think it over.

A kindly reminder. When your doctor says to keep active, it doesn't mean that you can do it anywhere!

17

Uhm

"Did you hear that, George? Franco will go to First Class."
Pause. "To First Class, did you get that George? To find the
Swarovski watch with the white ceramic strap that I absolutely
adore!"

"Uhm," grumbles George, lost in his book.

I had already noticed the lady's robust wrist, there is no
way the watch can fit her. One of those wasted trips for the sake of
peace. I give it to her. No doubt that poor watch is running out of
time!

The passenger, against all odds, manages to put her hand
through the strap and asks, "Franco would you be so kind as to
help me close it? I know I have an 'important' wrist, but I want to
show it to George."

Moved by George's keen interest, I decide to help her,
hoping not to cut off the blood supply to her hand. Mission partly
accomplished.

"George, what do you think? Nice? Beautiful? Or simply…
unique?"

George does not utter a word, first he looks at me sorrily,
then he stares at her with a sharky look in his eyes and answers
with his multipurpose monosyllable, "Uhm."

George, this is a multiple question! You will never get away with just a 'Uhm'.

"George, I'll buy it, I absolutely adore it!"

George, without getting his eyes off the book and carrying on reading, asks her, "Do you really need it?"

"Oh, George stop it! Fork over your card and carry on reading, you grumpy old miser!"

Time is up! The strap is no longer able to cope with that VIW (Very Important Wrist), a link breaks and the watch flies off in a sort of slow motion. I twist and try to catch it, but I fail miserably. The watch lands on the head of a passenger three rows in front.

"Thank you, you are a darling. I'll buy it anyway. I will take it to my jeweller's, he will repair it. Come on George, give me your card."

"I'm sorry ma'am. I can't sell it to you, it's damaged. Don't worry, it's not a problem, but I can't sell you a faulty item."

"Don't you too start now; I WANT TO BUY IT! Today you are all conspiring against me, what's wrong with you? George doesn't talk to me; he doesn't give me his card and now you don't want to sell the bloody watch to me. George, are you mad at me? He doesn't listen to me on purpose. He's vengeful! Like that time, I was picking my tooth in the car and he suddenly slammed the brakes on to hurt me. I had blood all over my mouth and then he didn't want to stop!"

I have a broken watch in my hands, George doesn't want to part with his card, and she is not giving up.

"Enough!" shouts George. "If I could brake, I would do it right here on this plane! But for now, just take my flipping card and we'll sort this out later at home…"

"What do you mean at home, George? It's just £180, you pay and that's all sorted!"

18

Tatiana's Fungi

"Sit down and I shall talk to you in the language of wolves," exhorts the arcane *babushka* from behind her miracle stall at *Zelyiony Bazar* (Green Bazar) in Almaty.

"Talk to me in Russian; we'd be lucky if we understood each other this way, believe me."

"Ah ah ah! You speak Russian better than my grandmother; do as I say, sit down and give me your hand. You've been staring at my herbs for far too long, I am a forest doctor, I speak the language of wolves and I fly with bats."

Why not? After all, a forest doctor is a shaman and someone talking to wolves can't be any worse than somebody dancing with them. Even so, we do have something in common, I fly too!

"Mario, take this birch fungus, she says it's better than a radiator; it'll keep you company…"

With Mario sorted, I can now concentrate on the mysterious she-werewolf/shaman. She tells me she's Russian and not Kazakhstani. She lives in the Ural forests and three months a year she comes to Almaty's market to sell her goods.

"Let's put a hand on each other's forehead and feel one another," Tatiana orders categorically.

Avatar moment.

"You haven't got prostate cancer."

"…Did you say 'have' or 'haven't'?"

Tatiana, I didn't think you would come out of the gate running like that; could you not hold your horses a bit longer and highlight your negations, please? If I accidentally missed a 'not', that could give me a heart attack!

"Your brain is still as good as new, but at the moment you are stranded!"

Actually, yes, the radar of our ancient 767 has broken down and this is why we got stuck in Almaty three days ago. It all makes sense!

"Back home, they are waiting for you… but it's not as if they were walking on hot bricks."

That's also true. Our Gedeone is not a worrier, I am the one who should be worried because that bloody feline hasn't pressed a single 'Like' on my Facebook posts for days!

"You are in good health; you don't need my herbs. Franco, stand up and have a wander around this beautiful market with your friend. Ask him to carry around the *chaga*, he can't read, he does not speak our language (whose language? Do you understand that it's not mine either? And why on earth should one be carrying around a birch fungus to feel less lonely?). It will help him to communicate in these parts. When you come back to this neck of the woods, if you have a headache or just feel like having a cup of tea, do stop by, I am a bridge woman, you should know it by now."

I went around the market, together with Mario and his birch fungus, and I felt wonderfully at home here too, in Central Asia, surrounded by a kaleidoscope of colours, shapes and mixed people. A crossroads between East and West, North and South, amidst slanted eyes and Tartar cheekbones; each person an ethnographic museum! A nice little haven. An enchanted world.

"So, is this the navel of the world then, the famous permanent centre of gravity?"

"Da!" confirms Mario, munching on a fragment of Tatiana's *chaga*. I can't disturb him; he is in talks. He resumes bargaining for a bunch of out-of-season cherries with Irina. Now the price has plummeted to 3000 Tenge per kilo.

Ah! The communicative power of Tatiana's birch fungi...

19

On Golden Pond

"Please, give me one more Bacardi & Coke, I'll promise you, this is my last. I'll have it, fall asleep and wake up in Frisco!"

"The agreement was that the last one I gave you was going to be THE last one, do you remember?"

"No."

Unwilling to understand but always willing to want. I'll try to ignore him, sooner or later he will give up.

"Come on mate, just one more, my VERY last one!"

What a bore! There is only a certain number of things I can pretend I have to do.

"If you don't give me one more drink, I'm gonna have to pee!"

Hold on a minute, this is a non sequitur! It's not allowed. Why does he only need to go for a pee if I don't give him a drink? I'm missing something here. I won't turn around, but I'm not deaf. Meanwhile, a 6-foot-something beanpole takes out his shlong, opens his locks, and floods the galley!

"What are you doing?"

"I won't stop 'til you give me another Bacardi & Coke!"

"You won't stop!? You can't just irrigate our galley willy-nilly!!!"

On an aircraft, tools are limited. I try to come up with something. Shall I take a megaphone and try to talk directly to the 'little' fella hoping that the vibration stops urination, or shall I get a jemmy and hit the big fellow on the head?

Meanwhile, the (in)continent(al) drift carries on. It just occurs to me that he is travelling with a group of soldiers. I go fetch his friend, a 7-foot musclehead.

"Sergeant!"

"I've just had a wee-wee, soldier!"

The Cyclops crosses the golden pond, lifts his superior like a rag doll and takes him to his seat. "I do apologise," he says. "When he sobers up, I'll give him a good beating, I imagine that now you won't serve us any more booze, am I right?"

Don't ask me who drained the golden pond in the galley, some experiences are better lived only once!

20

The Wow Factor

"Thank you for being here today. You are our future; the airline is investing in you!"

Is it a no-repayable loan? They are no longer just looking for volunteers, they really want us, only us, nothing but us! How can one not feel the love?

"Our surveys tell us that passengers in Business Class can no longer sleep as they wish, and they don't eat the way they would like. In short, the WOW factor seems to be missing from our premium cabin! That's why we have designed this course; to improve our service in Business is crucial for our survival. Today, you'll be our passengers, we will amaze you with our new service routine, already tried and tested by Turkish Airlines. It runs so smoothly and so wonderfully. Tomorrow, it will be your turn to surprise us by delivering the WOW factor!"

"You'll introduce yourselves to every single passenger as soon as they come on board, like they do in any restaurant."

Not at the restaurants I normally hang out. It only happens in the USA and for the one and only reason: gratuities (tips on this side of the Atlantic). But on board they are not allowed, so?

"You will say something along the lines of, 'Welcome on board. My name is Franco, I'll be working in this cabin on your flight to San Francisco. If you need anything, this is the call bell to get my attention. Have a pleasant flight.'"

But that's just asking for trouble!

"Mario, is Gede ok? Can we not go home? Why are they investing in us against our will? Can't we just sign our lives away in Economy for the rest of our career?"

"I've already signed on the dotted line, but they didn't take any notice. We are doomed to work in the new enhanced Business Class. We'll just have to bite the bullet; we are the chosen. The new sky dervishes."

"Et voilà! This is the new étagère that you'll use on the trolley... do you like it? Admit it, it's got that WOW factor, hasn't it just?" our trainer asks, proudly showing us a sort of shelving unit overflowing with all good things.

"Fucking what? What's a bloody EETAJAY? Excuse my French?" Jennifer rebuts. Does she want to be excused for her literal or euphemistic French?

"Passengers will be able to choose more than one starter from the étagère and you will no longer need to describe the choices to them, they will see them with their very own eyes thanks to this sublime presentation. As you know, an image is worth more than a thousand words!"

"And how about our sleeve wine carrier? Genuine Italian leather! *Magnifico!* Di-wine, rather, isn't it?" adds the other trainer while whizzing through the cabin with a sort of udder hanging from her arm 'nestling' two bottles of wine.

Only on the ground, there is no WOW factor due to turbulence, though.

"This will allow you to offer your passengers both white and red wine in one swipe without having to compromise on style. Never underestimate the power of the WOW factor!"

"Moving on. Desserts. How many times, let's be honest, did you find yourselves in the sticky situation where you had to refuse a second helping to a sweet-toothed passenger? Or, come on, you can come clean now, how many times did you run out of hot desserts on a New York because there were only five or six loaded? Problem solved. Now, they will have four desserts to choose from as well as a cheese board fit for a king. As usual, if they choose to have cheese, you must offer them a glass of Port. Remember, a need anticipated in time sends them to cloud nine!"

"Which brings us to glasses. Please pay attention! The cut-glass tumbler is used for water - with a slice of lemon if sparkling, no ice nor lemon if still -, juices – including tomato – and any other soft drinks. The bullet tumbler is for champagne or welcome cocktails and it must be filled to the brim. The oval-shaped is for red and white wines but not for rosé…"

"Mario, it's as clear as mud to me! Do you remember the Nutella drinking glass from our childhood? Everything was so simple back then! What did you drink in it? A little bit of everything, didn't you? Just saying…"

"It might all look very complicated right now. But let's not get bogged down with too many details. Rest assured; you will learn how to juggle the new glassware in no time! As the saying goes, the winner breaks them all, sorry… practice makes perfect!"

Second day. Time to swap roles!

Our trainers become passengers and we have a go at the new WOW inspiring service. It's a little bit like playing Of Guards and Thieves: it doesn't really matter what role you choose, sooner or later what goes around comes around, it's the circle of life... karma chameleon...

"Come on guys! Are you ready to amaze us?" our trainers spur us from their seats. "And don't forget the WOW factor!"

I go out into the cabin, I introduce myself to every single passenger, I take their coats, I tell them where they can find the call bell button (Suicidal!), I explain the service routine and what to expect. In other words, I endeavour to do my best to follow the new service standards. If we are good, we might go home earlier!

By the way, did I feed the cat?

"I'd like to taste a different red wine. Which one would you recommend?" asks me an ever more demanding passenger.

I know what to do! I go back to the galley, grab the wine udder, and return into the cabin in perfect gaucho style with two bottles hanging from my aching left arm. Not enough WOW factor. I try to think how to sweep my passengers off their feet. Maybe I should carry a candied cherry on the tip of my nose while dancing through the cabin like a Bolshoi ballerina, asking passengers what they would like to drink. I could astound passengers by turning into a performing seal!

"I'd like a glass of rosé."

WTF! Glassware nightmare. I have about four different kinds of glasses in the galley, which one is it for rosé? The oval one? No. The suppository-looking one? Nah. The bullet doesn't inspire me. I go for the Sue Ellen style and hope for the best!

"That's all folks! Exercise over. Thank you all very much! Fab. You really have captured the spirit of the new Business Class! Our passengers - but we should actually say, our passengeresses, because as you might know, female passengers have overtaken male passengers – love to be pampered, to be waited on hand and foot. We don't expect you to tuck them in (*maybe next year*), but you can always cover them if you notice that their duvet has gone askew while they sleep. Paying attention to small details like these can make a world of difference to them. Well done! Give yourselves a good old pat on the back! You proved to us that the company was right to invest in you. Now you can go out there and amaze them like you did with us today. Bravo!"

"Mario, did you do the seal number on your side?"

"What seal number?"

"Forget it! It was just something that went through my mind. I'll tell you later."

WOW!

21

Mental Health Is Priceless, For Everything Else...

"Hi, my name is Mary," mutters an American forty-something lady who has walked all the way from Business Class to the back of the plane with a pillow under her arm.

The usual sleepless passenger in the mood for a chat?

"Hi, Mary, I'm stuck on 4 down. Are you good at crosswords?"

"Yes... Are you alone? Where are your female colleagues?"

"They're all on their break apart from Audrey. I have already tortured her enough, but she hasn't got a clue about 4 down. Mary, come on, I'm counting on you!"

"Well, I'm from New York... I don't like Baltimore..."

I guess she is not very interested in my crosswords. Truth be told, I think she doesn't give a damn.

"Anyway, if Audrey doesn't come back soon, you'll have to help me. I need 'to spend a penny' as you say in London, England," she adds.

I don't grasp the connection between my colleague and Mary's urge to use the toilet but thank God I can see Audrey heading back to the rear galley; they will understand each other. That's what women do; they always go to the loo together! I make myself scarce, I pretend to concentrate on 4 down but eavesdrop everything.

"Hi Audrey, I came from Business Class because there are only male flight attendants in that cabin. I'm claustrophobic… and need to use the restroom, I can't lock myself in. Now, let me explain what I'll do. I will wedge this pillow in the folding door, and I would need you to be so kind as to stay outside and make sure nobody comes around, is that ok? Don't worry, I always do it in NYC as well when I catch a taxi. I wear a yellow raincoat and leave a piece of my belt trapped in the door; I feel much safer this way. I'd never be able to stay *all* in. I do the same with my skirt, the only problem is that sometimes it gets trashed. But it doesn't really matter, my mental balance is priceless."

"Don't worry! In the meantime, I'll carry on reading my *Hello Magazine*," Audrey reassures her.

Mary gets into the toilet, crushes the pillow in the door and hopefully she manages to relax.

"Audrey?" asks Mary. "Can you hear me? You aren't looking, are you?"

"No, I'm turned the other way," Audrey answers rolling her eyes.

"Turn around and tell me if you can see me."

After an endless 'Can you see me? Can you hear me? Turn around, turn the other way' and 'No, I can't see you, it's ok, I'll turn the other way', I give up finishing my crosswords.

"There's no signal in the toilets, Mary, don't worry. No one can see you, but they are under video surveillance, so you can

Sky Almighty ·   98

wave 'hello' to the flight crew. The camera is right behind the mirror!" I shout from the galley.

It serves you right for not helping me with 4 down!

Next time you go to New York, while waiting at a red light on 5th Avenue, if you see a piece of fabric fluttering from a yellow taxi, don't be rude. Say hello to her, you already know her name.

HAIL MARY!

22

Faith Tourism

Flight to Jedda. Faith tourism.

The Economy Class cabin seems a chessboard: white pilgrims on one side and black neophytes on the other. Well, quite a remarkable matroneum and patroneum, except that men wear a two-piece gown, a sort of unmatched bathrobe they just can't nonchalantly show off. I understand that some of them are not used to it, but this is the moment they've always dreamt of; Mecca is getting closer and closer, a little dignity, please!

And if the mountain won't come to Muhammad... then Muhammad must fly to the mountain.

They perambulate the cabin as if walking precariously on the balance beam; some sport easy wear tunics, Islam always meets everybody halfway. Others use a Velcro fastener to join the two pieces of cloth on the chest and a hook on the side for the little skirt. Fraying all over, not one single hem; pilgrim fashion through and through.

The back galley has morphed into the Wanderer Tailor's Shop; my colleague and I are busy trying to fix the children of Allah, attempting to conceal flabby bellies, wrapping their large bodies in presentable nappy-looking robes, holding them together with safety pins to hide their hirsute chests. Some of them admit that, despite being Muslim, it's the first time they dress up like that - or down, depending on how you look at it - but so it is written and so it must be done; they must be the closest resemblance to Mohammad during the Hegira.

While I am struggling to baste his tunic, Abdullah asks, "May I go to the loo?"

"Of course, just push the door in the middle, but you're still provisional. Helen will fix things properly when you come back, alright?"

"Yes, I need to go, it's urgent."

This was the last time we saw him in two pieces.

He quickly comes out and the little skirt gets stuck in the folding door, but he doesn't notice it straight away; no, he marches on towards the galley with his little cape over the shoulders and down below… almost nothing.

"Abdullah… your little skirt got stuck in the door, would you like me to fetch it for you?"

"Noooooo! I'll get it myself; stay where you are. Has someone seen my underwear?"

"No, Abdullah; you and I are the only two people in the galley!"

"Tell me the truth, you saw my briefs!"

I swiftly change the subject and I ask him to talk to me about Haj, the Mecca pilgrimage, how it works, how long he's been planning this journey. Nothing. The tongue ever turns to the aching tooth.

"What colour are my briefs?"

"Oh, drat! What can I say… generally white!"

So pushy! He asked for it.

"Ehm… just so you know, I woke up at 4 o'clock this morning, so it means I've been wearing them since the crack of dawn and on top of it, it's been a very emotional day; I'm doing things I've never even considered in my life. What do you think? It's one of Islam's five pillars, no joke, you know!"

One hour to landing, we have just entered Saudi's air space and a metamorphosis in reverse is taking place. On the other aisle, the neophytes, accompanied by their mothers, are being harnessed appropriately. Fatima is cocooned up from head to toe. Her mother takes her to the toilet, and we see her coming out completely covered up, but with a sort of circle around her head… a bumper, rather. And Fatima, giggling away, is groping around towards the galley, like a blind hen.

"I put a visor under the veil to try and create a beam of light, she's not used to *hijab*; I have to take her to Mecca, I need her all covered up, but she must have some light underneath. She can hardly manage to walk looking straight ahead," she explains to my colleague. "She finds it difficult to walk like that. Fatima, don't look down, look straight ahead; I just put the visor to help you a bit, don't stare at your feet otherwise you'll bump into something."

You might not be born a Muslim; however, you will hardly become one on board an aircraft!

23

The Double-Barrelled Waste no Time

"Young man, is it on yet?" Mrs Fitz-Gander asks me from her reclined seat, two fake cucumber slices on her eyes and her face turned heavenward.

That was to be expected. During boarding, her daughter introduced her as Lady Fitz-Gander, warning us to address her by her noble title and entrusting us also with her hat that, more than an item of headwear, looked like a happy compromise between an RSPB natural oasis and a fruit and vegetable stall: a huge Saturn with plumes of a variety of feathered friends, bunches of grapes, figs, pomegranates, and countless yards of tulle; now I know what they mean when certain ladies complain their head is spinning.

On the passenger list, next to the Lady's name, the message was clear:

In serenity

which for outsiders means 'venerable old woman' or 'old bag', whichever comes to mind first. I don't know how to answer the crock, so holding my bar trolley, I look quizzically at her daughter who wins the on-the-spot prize for facial expressions of the year, 'Say yes!'

I play along, hopefully only for a little while.

"Of course, Lady Fitz-Gander."

"See, mum? I told you that in Economy Plus they turn on UV tanning lamps straight after take-off," announces boastfully her daughter, staring at the individual overhead reading lights. Then she reassures her shouting in her ear, "Anyway, you can tell them if it is too hot, they can turn it down. You haven't been to THE BAHAMAS for over a year (did you all hear that?), you'd better start to get used to the scorching sun of the Caribbean WHERE WE HAVE OUR VILLA (did you all hear where they are going and whose villa it is?)."

Hold on a minute.

Are you telling me that her daughter is making the old prune believe that we offer an inflight UV tanning service in Economy Plus because she didn't want to buy her a Business Class ticket?

"It feels a bit hot; would you please be so kind as to give me my handbag? I'm desperate for some face cream."

I'm getting hot under the collar, I still have a whole bar service to do and the hoary lady is holding me hostage and asks me to rummage through her ointments, lotions and royal jelly jars in her beauty case. You can't find a snake bite serum for love or money!

I feel like making an announcement, I must calm down, I desperately need a harpist, even a graduating one would do, who can play the Intermission Song for me.

I can't believe my eyes! At a cruising altitude of 37,000 feet, is double-barrelled Lady Fitz-Gander, with her seat reclined in the dentist position, two plastic cucumber slices over her eyes and Estee Lauder cream on her face, really convinced she's under a tanning lamp??? And her daughter, can't she tell her that, by comparison, the skin of an armadillo seems that of a new-born baby?

Permission to land, please!

24

Xmas Eve

"Ma'am, I will accompany you to your seat, just take my arm," I tell the lady who has just arrived at the door in a wheelchair.

"I'd take your whole body as a Christmas present, darling!"

Lesson learned. Next time just offer an inch, they always go for the mile anyway...

After take-off.

Ding, ding, ding!

I don't feel like standing up, and by the way, the fasten-seatbelt sign is still illuminated. The call bell does not stop, this is turning into tintinnabulation! Despite the aircraft still skyrocketing like a pirate ship, I stand up and answer that call.

"Could I have the Xmas Cocktail, please?"

Hold on a minute, what cocktail is he talking about and can't he see that no human should be walking around? I am here just because as cabin crew I must be superhuman!

I frown at him. There is no need to tell him that we forgot our cocktail umbrellas in Mumbai, he gives up on his request of his own free will.

"What's for Xmas lunch?" he carries on as if we could go back in case he doesn't fancy it.

"It's Christmas Eve, no meat as per religious prescription," I reply making it up. I turn around and go back to my jump seat.

Today, passengers will not have my sculp; they will not eat me alive with a side dish of roasted potatoes!

Two hours later, London is getting closer and closer.

...And your flight shall never end, He booms from above.

Really?

Ding, ding, ding... another call bell. Tonight, passengers are really in a jingling mood!

I get up to 42A. Mouth wide open, call bell light on.

"No, *I* pressed the call bell," admits 42B. "I think he has problems in closing his mouth. He's been like this, with his mouth wide open, for over half an hour. Can anything be done to stop his 'astonishment'?"

Such as...

Maybe he's like that because he saw Santa Claus out of the window shooting through the sky pulled by Dasher, Dancer, Prancer and all the rest. My jaw would drop as well if this were the case! Why do you always ask for solutions that I don't have?

But first, what's the problem? He might have taken some jaw-dropping, stoning drugs...

The 'astonished' passenger tries to gesticulate and I think he wants to tell me that everything is ok with him, but I find it

Sky Almighty · 110

difficult to believe him… at least he's got tonsillitis by the look of it.

"HA – HA – HAL," moans Bigmouth.

For Goodness sake, what is he trying to tell me? A telegram would be clearer!

"I know, we've tried to speak to him, but I don't understand what he's saying. He doesn't articulate very well, does he? That's why I pressed the call bell, because I'm not sure, but I think he needs help, you must know what to do."

"HA-HA-HAL, HA-HA-HAL, HA-HA-HAL, HALLLL," he mutters, but I can't crack his prosody: short syllable, long syllable, caesura, caesura, short, long, short, long… As far as I'm concerned, he could be singing *Twinkle, Twinkle, Little Star*… I give up, but by his gesticulating I glean he wants a pen and a piece of paper.

End of the Charades.

He gives me the note where he has written in big letters, "PA-NA-DOL. JAW LOCKED!" So, Santa has nothing to do with it. This must be a pre-existing condition. When this happens at home, he probably takes a muscle relaxer, but today paracetamol will have to do. Thank God, because on board we don't have much more than that. I get him a paracetamol, a glass of water and an eye mask to cover his gaping maw.

Within an hour, that paracetamol manages to work wonders…

"TH – K – U."

Sometimes they are grateful.

About an hour later.

Ding, ding, ding!

Now, for whom does the call bell toll?

An Indian lady fainted on the floor. I call my colleague immediately and we raise her legs. It must be the usual case of low blood sugar. They normally recover very quickly. Except her!

"Let's take her to Business Class so she can lie down on the seat," I suggest.

We seek to gather more information amid the sobbing of an elderly lady wearing a sari, who must be her mother, and her little daughter sitting next to her. We ask the usual questions.

"Does she have any allergies?"

"Any specific condition that we should be made aware of?"

"Does she have diabetes?"

"Has she had it before?"

Regardless of what they tell me, my reaction is always more or less the same, 'Ah!' uttered with a mixture of surprise and professionalism. I write everything down on a form because we must radio our medical team in Phoenix from the cockpit.

"Ma'am, have you got any pain?" I ask as soon as she opens her eyes.

"Yes, I feel like I have an elephant crushing on my chest, it's like a burning feeling."

TA – TA – TA – TAN!

I tell Mario to go and get me the defibrillator at once.

"Of course, she has a burning feeling in the chest," remarks the little girl, about seven years of age. "It's all that food that we had at our relatives' in India! I prefer Taco Bell or Mexican burritos. Mom, throw everything up and promise me that you will never ever take me to India again!"

We put the mother on oxygen, I sit down on the stool in front of her with her legs on my knees. The grandmother has tears rolling down her face, the little girl nestled next to her.

"I feel the same when I eat Indian food, it's so spicy that it makes me cry and then I need to blow my nose; it burns on the way in and on the way out for that matter," she tells me holding her mother's hand.

"Don't worry, your mom will digest everything, and she will be fine," I reassure her.

Since, by the look of it, this year we won't have a white Christmas, I'm just telling a few white lies.

"Anyway, I want to be a Science teacher when I grow up, so someone must tell me where the oxygen in this little tube comes from because I can't see it."

"Can you see that little green mark in the tube? It means oxygen is flowing; when it's red it means oxygen is off."

"But who turns it on?"

"The captain from the flight deck, but for now just hold your mum's hand and leave science alone…"

And above all, leave ME alone... I'm trapped here while I should be on my break.

"I want to control it, I want to see what happens to her if I turn it off," says the little girl getting dangerously close to the oxygen outlet above the seat.

Goodness gracious me! Can anyone take away this little pest who wants to play science while her mother is having a suspected heart attack?

Ding, ding, ding!

The little girl presses the call bell. My colleague arrives.

"Franco, do you want me to take over from you?"

"No, he stays where he is. I'm sick, I ate the same shitty food my mom had at my uncle's. I need oxygen as well!" she says while faking fainting.

"Victor, bring me a bottle of oxygen, I'll make sure she sees the guiding star!" I feel like hitting the snotty kid on the head but then again, she might have a future as a Science teacher.

At 04.46 GMT, on Christmas Day, the mother lets out a resolutive Yeti belch that dispels any doubt.

"See, I told you!" proclaims the little Science teacher sticking her tongue out.

25

Past the Age of Consent

"Then, if need be, would you help me spoon-feed him?"

"Yes, of course, have a look at the menu, I'll be back in a minute to take your order."

The man stares at me with a shallow gaze and would like to tell me something.

"No!" his wife exclaims. "You naughty little thing! You shouldn't even be thinking about that!"

But when you are 80 plus, at least freedom of thought should be guaranteed, should it not?

"An aub..." and the rest dies on his lips. I'll never know what he was trying to tell me and meanwhile his shaky little hands head further south.

"Stop it! He hasn't got it."

What about if I did have it and would like to please him?

Here I am in front of my passengers for the safety demonstrations in the other cabin.

"How lovely! The cabin is half empty. I think about the usual and smile. They are going to sleep, aren't they? At this time of night, nobody is going to want to eat, otherwise, what's the point of lounges at the airport?

"I can't hear the demonstrations. Can you tell her to stop chatting?" a passenger on the left aisle asks, indicating the lady on the opposite aisle.

I encourage the woman to pay attention. She obeys visibly upset. She stands up, lifts her blouse, and flashes her assets to the man.

"Has the gentleman's hearing improved at all now?"

Why are you distracting me, I wonder, when I am mentally preparing my shopping list? I am trying to defuse the situation by anticipating slightly the pointing of the emergency exits; the gentleman on the other aisle is obviously confused. In all honesty, a half striptease during the safety demonstrations is a first for me, I'll just pretend it never occurred. Was the lady by any chance showing the flotation buoys in case of ditching?

"They are on me!" shouts a passenger sitting in the vicinity of the shameless lady.

Something does not add up.

"Mr Simpson?"

"Exactly!"

They adore it when a stranger calls them by their surname, they look at you as if you'd read it on their forehead. I scroll the passenger list and I read the message next to his name, 'No dinner, strange attitude, must sleep.'

Ah, our ground staff colleagues are getting more cryptic by the flight. Does it mean that he is strange because he refused to dine, or am I supposed to punish him by sending him to bed without supper? I'd better ask.

"Mr Simpson? You are not going to dine tonight, right?"

"No."

"The lady on the other side of the aisle is your wife, is she not?"

"Yes. Did you like the peep show? I paid for them!"

I chuckle a little, but I don't want to pass for an opportunist.

"And what about your wife, is she going to have dinner?"

"I don't know, I'm just her bill footer. She doesn't even speak to me; I am afraid you're going to have to ask her. Can't you see? She only has eyes for that gentleman next to her, she hasn't stopped throwing herself at him since they were in the lounge."

I have just remembered that in the other cabin there's someone who needs spoon-feeding.

I security check the left aisle as well and I notice that the gentleman who had demanded silence in the cabin looks at me quizzically, he's looking for confirmation.

"But I had only asked the woman to be quiet… I'd have never expected she'd show me all that jazz."

"What jazz?" I ask him, pretending nothing ever happened.

"The jazz that he paid for," he continues pointing at the husband on the other aisle.

"Anyway, did you understand where the emergency exits are?" I test him.

"No, I got distracted, but should there be an emergency, I'd follow her to the ends of the earth; I'm sure she knows a few nice little places where to go."

I don't even want to know what he's talking about and before take-off I have to solve the 'aub...' puzzle in the other cabin.

"Have you decided what you want to eat?"

"Yes, for me, tortellini with tomato sauce and for him... anything goes."

He tries to finish off the sentence he had left open.

"...ergine, have you got it?" he asks with his hand right on the lap.

"Dirty old man! You and that little filthy mind of yours! Don't take any notice, young man, sorry, he's totally out of his mind. That was a game we used to play nearly a decade ago.... when we were still jaunty and bouncy."

Well, could you explain to me, just out of curiosity, what you were doing, aged 70, with an aubergine?

I'll go back to Economy to see what stage we are at with the strip show. Thank goodness, there are no poles around.

26

The Eye of the Desert

"It was her, the raspberry headed with cropped hair! She pushed my seat back and now I have a dislocated shoulder. I need medical attention; perhaps the police should get involved!"

The African Celia Black, with her crimson eyebrows sitting in the row behind, lifts her hands to the sky in surrender: she has nothing to do with the accident, and the lady next to her confirms it. I tell them all off: the dislocated and her neighbour, the cropped and her travelling companion, hoping to find a quick solution that makes everybody happy.

"No, my shoulder is just a distraction, how can I explain it to you?" and with her finger she invites me to kneel next to her. "Have you ever heard of the Eye of the Desert?" she whispers into my ear. "That humongous 30-mile circle in Mauritania? You know what I'm talking about (Maybe she does but I honestly don't), have we already passed it?"

"We should be flying over it in the next ten minutes."

"I knew it!!! Anyway, they are not like us; we are Liberians and they are Mauritanians, understand? Those with cropped raspberry hair and bloody eyebrows are the worst!"

Well, there are quite a few ginger-haired in Europe too. They can't be punished just for that!

"I can't doze off with them sitting in the row behind! Can you see that bag? It contains a spray and everything they need! If I stay awake… maybe… but I'm pretty sure they got that awful spray, made from a Chinese insect, and they make you numb… next thing you know, all your hair is gone!"

"Well, but you don't agree with that, do you?"

"I knew you wouldn't understand. You Europeans know nothing about these things!"

The story in its absurdity is becoming rather interesting.

"Of course, I don't want them to chop off my hair! But they've got razors in that bag. Two minutes and you are bald, that's all they need! And then, how can you prove that you weren't already like that? And do you know what they do with that hair when we fly over the Eye of the Desert?"

"Yes, I think it is rather terrible." I pretend to sympathise with her since understanding is impossible.

"Take a picture of me without them seeing you! A picture of my full head of hair! That's the only hope left I have, so I can report them. Take a picture of them as well, and then when I come back to Africa, I will take it to my village chief, he might be able to help. Anyway, my hair is gone, believe you me! I hope they leave my eyebrows in peace!!!"

"But do you think that they are such skilled barbers that no one is going to notice, not even you? And where do they keep all those deadly tools?"

"I have no time to explain. Have you taken the pictures? Soon we will be flying over the Eye. Now there is nothing I can do, look at my hair for the last time… It will take me years to regrow it!!!"

"But if you like, I can move you to a different seat."

"No, it will make no difference!"

I've got half a mind to sit next to the Liberian lady and sacrifice my own hair, at the end of the day I could do with a trim!

27

Barking Mad

"Now the Black Panther is all yours!"

"But had she not been banned from flying for…"

"Ban expired, I'm afraid!"

Oh, bloody hell… when??? I thought she could never set foot in the skies again. A least, have her nails been capped?

On this sad note, the dispatcher gives me the thumbs up to close the door. But I already knew from the passenger list that today in First Class, in 1A, we had the One&Only Black Venus. But thank God, I'm not working in First, so I won't have to worry about the rebel model.

I quite fancy an Earl Grey though, so I head fore.

Fatal mistake.

"Why don't you spray some insecticide?" asks me the panic-stricken Catwalk Queen.

"We only do it when we travel to and from certain destinations, in Africa and the Far East, according to WHO's guidelines."

"Don't you know that New York is teeming with tiger mosquitoes?"

I feel in danger, her claws are out; I must find a tiger mosquito swatter otherwise she's going to disfigure me. This is a fight for survival!

"Do you know whether my seat has been sanitised?"

"I'll find out for you."

The worst is over, I'll never drink Earl Grey for the rest of my life; I pass the buck to my colleagues working in First and I hole up in Business Class while the panther is dealing with tiger mosquitoes and cleaning the armrests with a sort of magic ointment. But today, I'm not having a good day...

Ding, ding

"I'd like two sachets of sweetener; my Diet Coke is too bitter. Can I also have a teaspoon to give it a stir?"

That makes perfect sense! If you cut sugar with one hand, you must add it with the other, and since you like the bubbling effect, you also need a teaspoon ...

But I'm paid to smile.

"He doesn't let anyone in," my colleague informs me out of breath, coming up to Business Class where she would never set foot if it weren't for a life-or-death emergency. This doesn't bode well, there's definitely going to be trouble ahead.

"But who?"

"The old boy, the one who wanted to sleep in the bassinet."

Something does not add up. I must go and have a look.

Who would have thought? A big guy is standing in front of a toilet in Economy with his arms crossed.

"Morning," I start off, just to break the ice.

"Nobody wants it anymore!" he says showing me a toilet paper roll.

"Yes," a passenger expands, "he's asking everybody if we want some toilet paper and if we say no, he doesn't allow us to use the loo! Who is he? We are desperate for a wee-wee!"

Well, I haven't got a clue who he is, but by what he's doing I think we're heading for disaster.

"On this plane, too much toilet paper is wasted!" states the chamberlain. "It's time to put an end to such waste, starting right now!"

A speech that at an election rally would make him mayor on the spot at the very least.

"Liquid evacuation, one sheet. Solids, two or three, it depends," he points out.

A flawless disquisition: he deserves a round of applause for his environmental awareness, but for us it turns into a difficult situation to manage.

"True!" I exalt. "We will proceed on a case-by-case basis!"

I will explain everything to the other passengers later. Trust me, I know what I'm doing.

"It's time to get some fresh air!" he declares grabbing the handle of Door 3 right.

"AHHHHHHHHH!!!!!" the whole terrorised cabin shouts.

"Don't worry, everything is under control."

So to speak...

Let's recap.

A giant - well into his seventies, and far beyond his expiry date - wants to sleep in a bassinet, authorises the use of the loo only with rationed toilet paper and tries to open the door of a Boing 777. And let's not forget that in First, the black panther is wearing a rhinoceros-looking mask while lying on her bed and spraying insecticide as if there were no tomorrow.

Emergency meeting in the front galley.

It's decided, the dodderer must be handcuffed before things get out of hand.

Time to assign the restraining plan roles.

"I'll be the handcuffer!" my colleague proclaims.

"I'll throw the blanket," I offer.

"I'll tie him up," ventures Mario the Brave.

Now that all the roles have been decided, it's time to spring into action.

Let Operation Blackbird begin!

What does it entail exactly? I should quietly approach the passenger from behind, throw the blanket on the head of the old chap who, taken by surprise and already in a fugue state, should raise his arms to try and free himself; at that very moment, my colleague, with her impeccable chignon, should handcuff him in just one move.

This is textbook handcuffing they teach us in training. But in real life, things can turn out quite differently.

Strange but true, I throw the blanket, he lifts his arms in the dark, my colleague with her angelic face handcuffs him and we sit him down. Now, it's spitting, biting and kicking time... Who ventured to tie him up to the seat?

Oh yes, Mario...

Lo and behold, the old guy breaks into tears.

"Please, don't tie me up! I'll be a good boy; I wouldn't hurt a fly anyway. All I wanted was lie down in the bassinet and a little bit of fresh air; you can't deny an elderly person some oxygenated air!"

My colleague, moved by his sweet face, rushes to the nearest oxygen bottle, Eva-Kent style. She comes back, turns it on and puts him on oxygen. The handcuffed grabs the bottle and smashes it across her shoulder.

"Auch!!!"

"Missed it. It was your head I was aiming for. You've got such beautiful hair!"

"Tie him up, please!!!" she implores while writhing in pain.

Mario, there's no getting away this time!

We eventually land in London. First Class is as toxic as Fukushima, all doors still safely closed, all toilets usable and the old man tied up to his seat. Now the police will investigate and come up with some answers. Meanwhile, a friendly *caveat*: always remember to take all your prescribed pills before boarding, and please, please, stick to the recommended doses!

28

Birthdays and Weddings by Proxy

And what about us cabin crew celebrating our birthdays at home once in a blue moon and the rest almost invariably flying over the high seas? Despite this, our birthdays come up regularly every year, like everybody else's, though.

This year, we almost managed a regular celebration.

There were 12 guests, they were young and strong and yes, they did not die, as the poem *The Gleaner of Sapri* by Luigi Mercantini would have it.

"Hello, this is Hong Kong calling Italy. My name is Franco and I booked a table for 30th May. Do you remember? We are the party that used to be of 10 people, then 11, then we went down to 6 but soared to 15 and eventually we stabilised at 14."

"Yes, I do remember; you are those who initially were supposed to come at 7 pm, then at 8 and eventually you're coming at 9.30."

"Exactly us, those who ordered vanilla panna cotta but then we changed it to strawberry and eventually we settled for a coffee one."

"Have you now changed your mind about your birthday?"

"No, I just wanted to let you know that the two birthday boys, Franco and Mario, are stuck in Hong Kong, I don't know whether you heard the news on TV, but here in Hong Kong there's a typhoon and the computer system is down at Heathrow and not one single flight is leaving at the moment."

"I see; but you, as cabin crew, will manage to fly somehow, won't you?"

Of course.

"Anyway, they'll celebrate for us. There are 12 of them and you are all authorised to open our presents."

"Can I keep them as well? You know, it's the first time we're having a birthday party by proxy. So, what shall we do? Are we going to video call you when we are about to cut the cake?"

"Perfect, with all the burning candles on it. With the two of us blowing, we should manage to have them out in no time! And the cake is on us, that's for sure."

"Yes?"

"Well, perhaps one of the guests can front the money…"

"Yes, one of the 12."

"And you're not going to believe this. In three days', my niece is getting married and we should be flying to the UK to fetch our suits and hitchhike from Wiltshire to Forlì – Italy. At the moment, Heathrow is carnage and no flights are departing."

"If I were you, I would dispatch the 12 apostles to the wedding too."

"You know what? I think this is a brilliant idea, you are a born problem solver. Thanks."

29

Yolanda

"Yolanda, Yolanda, how many years have you been flying, Yolanda?"

"39 and until my country is in such bad shape I think I will carry on ploughing the skies for quite a while," my Brazilian colleague replies and I am already addicted to her after only two minutes on board this aircraft bound for São Paulo.

"*Bom dia*, Yolanda, good luck to us. Boarding is starting, the beasts have been released."

Amidst a *direita*, an *ezquerda* and a *bem vindo*, at long last everyone is on. Lovely! While hopping around and slamming the overhead lockers to a tropical rhythm, I set my eyes on a crying lady staring at the void. I stoop to her level in the position of the Singapore Airlines' stewardess – 24/7 available, even when not in service – with all the empathy that's still in me at the beginning of every flight.

"Madam, is anything wrong?"

"Você fala português?"

With my 'carnival' Portuguese, I offer her a glass of water but she's still crying a river with no intention of stopping the flood. A bitter trickle is streaming down her chin, then her neck and eventually her blouse.

"Madam, are you a bit nervous for the flight?"

"No," her friend replies in English. "She's been in London for a year, she's crying with joy because she's going back home, perhaps she'll be fine in an hour or so. She's crying while smiling, can't you see?"

"Oh… Do people weep with joy for such a long time in Brazil?"

"Yes, tears of joy are the best thing that can happen to you," her friend adds with tears welling up in her eyes.

"Are you also crying with joy?"

"No, not me, I have a corn under my heel that's killing me," she replies in pain.

Actually, I should have known better, it was a totally different kind of weeping, more contrite and humbler.

I look around and I notice the general waterworks, I equip myself with glasses of water and plasters, I don't know what more I could do… besides, what's the first aid for someone crying their eyes out with joy?

Yolanda?

"If you don't mind, I'll put that bowl in the hat rack for take-off."

What the use of that family-size bowl might be escapes me.

"No, it will be full before you know it."

"What do you mean by full???"

"Yes, she's about to fill it up with vomit, that's why you might as well leave it down on the floor," her husband explains, pointing at his wife's swollen and extremely capacious belly.

"Listen, however abundant your wife's jet might be, a duty-free carrier bag should do the trick, shouldn't it? Let me put the bowl into the wardrobe for take-off, alright?"

"I can't guarantee, we have not travelled without a bowl for years; you can't even imagine how many times I had to change my car upholstery."

Ai, meu Deus!

Will we ever manage to lift this giant puddle of tears – joyous and sorrowful – up to the skies?

Departed.

I head for the galley after re-positioning the large bowl on the active volcano's lap.

On a full stomach, everything seems a lot quieter, tears have dried up, it almost feels like a normal flight.

"If I flush the toilet, the door wide-opens. Is it normal?"

No, certainly not, but the idea is so thrilling that I immediately put it to the test. Wow! It's really happening. When I push the 'flush' button, a magic vortex appears, making the door open wide!

Yolanda!

I explain the situation to my veteran Brazilian colleague who, rumours have it, hasn't set foot on the ground for nearly four decades.

"It only occurred to me once before, about 15 years ago," declares knowingly Yolanda, "I'm going to have to write a message on the door in Portuguese where I shall explain that when they flush, they must look presentable, so they can still carry on using it. I think this is the best way, otherwise there will be queues everywhere. It's no big deal!" She assures us that the message contains adequate instructions in her mother tongue and unexpectedly people start queuing up.

After reading the message, the first lady goes in, a bit nervous. Five minutes later, we hear the noise of the flush from the outside and a high-mountain cyclone forms at once. The lady re-appears with her Lily Savage hairdo, a sphinx look, and a passport smile. Looking proud of herself, she gives way to the next passenger in need. The toilet seems to have become a popular photo booth.

"Mum, what are you doing sitting on the throne? And what about that shawl around your neck, where did you get it from?"

Yes, not only do they not want to be caught out, after doing what they have to do, but before flushing, they even choose the best pose for the onlookers waiting outside. I am pretty sure that someone might have even tried to adjust the seat by swivelling it around to align their eyes with the 'NO SMOKING' sign.

Nobody wants to use the other toilets anymore; by now, the tornado opening has become the new inflight attraction and the queue is almost endless.

Yolanda???

30

Glass-eyed

"Let's see if we have anyone special on board today. I know that in their own small way they all are..." says the cabin manager in the briefing room scrolling down the passenger list. "Pretty usual stuff, apart from two ladies travelling with their dolls."

If fifteen cabin crew members, who have seen it all, look at you gaping, it means you must fill in the gaps.

"Nothing special, really. I just wanted to tell you because of our company's welcoming, inclusive, non-judgemental policy. Well, today, more than ever, I want you to show how open-minded and customer-oriented we are as an airline."

Sooner or later, he must come to the point...

The point.

"I think I'd better read out our ground colleagues' concise message to you. 'Pax travelling with two dolls they treat like real babies. Just accommodate their needs, no questions asked'."

Our fifteen-minute briefing must include safety and security, individual questions to ascertain our safety-and-emergency procedure knowledge; today, though, we would need an entire day to fully explore and understand 'the doll case', but we belong to the skies and it'll all be revealed to us once any terrestrial connection has been cut off and there is no turning back!

"I just wanted to inform you not because I don't trust your undeniable ability to deal with any situation, but to help you think a little out of the box, for some of you this experience might feel quite unusual. Don't ask me any question, this is all I know; but at the end of the day two dolls have never harmed anyone, right? *(What about Chucky, though?)* Well, thank you. Time's up, see you at Gate A32, and please, please, no duty-free shopping!"

We all stand up and leave the room visibly dazed.

"Christine, have you ever had it before?" I ask my slightly more senior colleague.

"What? No! I pretended I understood, but my only hope is that I won't be dealing with it, I wouldn't know where to look!" she answers candidly already in every-man-for-himself mode.

We go through Gate A32 and board the aircraft. I'm at the door for boarding with the cabin manager. "Why are they coming on in dribs and drabs today?" I ask him.

"We are nearly finished, only a couple more to come..." he answers vaguely.

We both know who he is referring to and deep down we both desire the same thing.

"Oh Lucy, come on darling, we are late," whispers to the doll the lady at the end of the jetty. "Lucy, those nice men are waiting for us! Look at that fella, he will cuddle and spoil you if you are a good girl!"

"Go and get her/them, otherwise we'll be here all day!" hums to me the cabin manager with a Hello-Magazine-Cover smile.

In the meantime, the second lady comes on board with John, the other doll who has a very happy face, eyes closed. I'm under the impression he won't be any trouble.

"She's never flown before. Maybe you know a way to convince her to get onboard. She loves lullabies! Do you mind trying to hold her in your arms and sing her something, anything really?" the mother asks me.

How can I possibly refuse to pursue my life-long dream? Saying no would mean to be responsible for delaying an entire 747!

"What's her name?" I ask her, just to personalise my performance.

"Lucy," she says with motherly pride while handing the little bundle of joy to me.

I'd better not look at that wrinkly little face with those staring glassy eyes. A true masterpiece of modern 'dollology'. I could lose my inspiration.

♫ *Rock-a-Bye Baby,*

On a treetop,

When the wind blows,

Lucy will drop. ♫

Wow! Perfect rhyming and while I'm singing 'Drop', I pretend to let Lucy fall to the ground, I kneel a little and she magically blinks!

"Look at the way she is staring at you! You little charmer! She only does that with men, you know… I think you've won her over! Cheeky little bugger!"

We get on board; I quickly close the door and answer the interphone.

"Are they all on? Dolls as well?" the captain asks me.

"Yes, all on board."

I stare at the handset in disbelief. It's getting ever more disturbing. I answered as if it was a technical question. What about if I had said 'No'? What would have happened? Would he have cancelled the flight?

I head towards Economy, both ladies are sitting by the window, one in front of the other, with their respective dolls, pardon, babies.

I take my statuary safety-demo position.

As if she had not already drawn enough attention while getting to her seat – rocking little Lucy while singing a lullaby –, the mother is now waving her arms asking for an extension seatbelt for the… doll! I reassure her with a smile. I gesticulate to tell her that I will get her one as soon as I'm done with the safety demos.

Passengers first stare at the mothers and then at us. I can feel their apprehension; our rehearsed nonchalance really unsettles them. I think they would like to get off, but we are already taxing out, too late!

I give her the extension seatbelt so that she can safely have Lucy on her lap for take-off. Passengers sitting nearby look at her with disdain and then they turn their eyes to me for some sort of approval and reassurance.

After take-off.

"Since you are here, would you mind taking this as well? You know, I don't want to disturb these people," she says while passing me a heavy-looking nappy.

"Yes, ma'am. Let me take it."

I can't resist, my curiosity is going through the roof. I must see with my very eyes what a doll can do. As soon as I'm away from prying eyes, I take a look… A concrete mixer would not have produced such huge amount! And what about this blackish-grey mire, what planet does it come from?

"Now, it would be mummy's turn to use the facilities. Would you mind holding her while I go to the restroom?"

"Of course not!"

"You be careful, she can be naughty, she might scratch you with those little nails of hers…"

I accept my predicament and with a Michelangelesque expression on my face I look around for someone's pity. My colleagues, even those with nothing left to do, pretend to be busy doing something and thank their lucky star for not having to work on my aisle. Mario, who is working on the opposite aisle, comes back to the galley, we make eye contact. We stare at each other. A moment of silent truth worth more than a thousand words. I need to let off steam and he knows it.

"Where is she?" he asks me.

"In the loo."

With his right index he makes a rotatory gesture authorising me to do what I would not have had the courage to initiate.

"Quick!" urges Mario.

"But… can I?" I hesitate.

"Of course!" he affirms.

As if under a spell, I hold Lucy by her little leg and give her a good spin into the air. Such a liberating and harmless merry-go-round!

"Stop!" warns Mario.

Just in time.

"Did she behave?" the mother enquires.

"An angel!" I reassure her.

"Before going back to my seat, can I ask you to warm up this for me, please?" she enquires, producing a baby bottle from one of the countless pockets of her 'nursing' apron.

"Yes, but it will take me at least five minutes. I need to immerse it in hot water, we don't have a microwave."

In other words… *Go back to your seat and leave me in peace for a while. I will bring it to you.*

"Don't worry, I'll wait here," she declares stubbornly, and starts to tell me the life and times of Lucy, the growing up doll.

"Ah, how interesting… she is very precocious. I think it's hot enough now."

"Since you're so kind, would you mind trying it on the back of your hand? I've just put on some moisturizer and maybe I can't feel the temperature alright."

I was born to be a sacrificial lamb…

"Not a problem."

I turn around and feel a few drops on the back of my hand.

SCORCHING!

My ears are nearly on fire. It did happen to me as a child when my mum used to give me mulled wine at Christmas.

"Perfect."

Now, I don't know what material they are made of, but dolls should have a melting point, shouldn't they? Finally, she decides to leave me alone with my Neronic dream and heads off the galley.

"So, we are going back to our seat now. If we need anything, we'll press the call bell that you love so much, my little Lucy, wont' we?"

One thing is for sure, I have reached my boiling or rather fuming point. I'm beside myself! I would need a little bit of privacy to have a bite to eat. I draw the curtains...

Too late!

A gadfly passenger flatters in.

"What a bore! Long-haul flights are definitely not my cup of tea. I don't know how you manage. I COULD NEVER DO YOUR JOB!"

We've heard it a million times before, but sometimes they even steal our trays to practice at home for future recruitment campaigns! Anyway, this lady is extremely dangerous; there is nothing worse than an insomniac passenger.

"Ma'am, you can sit down next to me, but do you mind if I carry on eating? You know, this is my... break."

Silence.

Having your dinner in silence with a stranger sitting next to you is bad enough, but when they start staring, that's when it becomes unbearable.

"Do you live in Charleston?"

"No, I was here for work. I came for a conference."

"Oh! What do you do?"

"I am a psychologist."

My dinner can wait!

I can't believe my luck. I make sure the curtains are completely drawn. I turn the galley into a professional therapeutic studio. I'm dreaming of lying down on a Freudian chaise longue while she analyses me.

"I think I need your professional expertise."

"It's not as bad as you think, trust me."

There is one thing I cannot stand about therapists: their capacity to explain the inexplicable as if it were the most natural thing in the world. But that's their job.

"You are bewildered at the two dolls, aren't you?"

Wow, she is really shrewd, I'll give her that!

"In Philadelphia as well, we have implemented the same protocol."

"Protocol?"

"Indeed. When lesbian couples feel a strong desire for motherhood, they come to us and we test their predisposition by providing them with a doll that they must treat in all respects like a real child. Desire and suitability do not always go hand in hand."

"But how do you monitor it?"

"This is where technology comes into play. Inside every single doll there is a microchip that detects and records... anything said..."

I'm no longer hungry.

"Any temperature variation..."

It wasn't that hot, was it?

"Any movement…"

The spinning… maybe wasn't such a good idea after all!

I pretend to pay attention by asking some technical questions.

"Oscillatory, undulatory, as well as rotatory movements?"

"Yes, even the slightest."

Mario, why did you make me do it?

"All this and much more. It's a very advanced and sensitive device. It's amazing how some 'wannabe mothers' while listening to their recordings realise that their desire for motherhood should remain in the realm of dreams. You look puzzled, Franco. Is everything alright?"

"Yes, just a little tired, that's all."

A few hours later while driving home.

"Mario, do you want to know the dolls' secret?"

"Go on then."

"Remember that lady I was talking to in the galley?"

"The woman wearing that purple hat?"

"Yes, her. She is a psychologist."

"And do you trust her?"

"Yes, why?"

"She told me that she is a convinced flat-earther."

"Doll therapy DOES exist, you know!"

"Yes, I know! But it's something else."

31

Torah, Nevi' m, Ketuvim and Sheitel

Characters:

Curly: Asher, orthodox Jewish husband

Wiggy: Rachel, Asher's wife

The steward: I, myself (maybe)

"Could you give me a big bottle of water?" Wiggy asks me.

"I can give you two glasses, ma'am. If you are still thirsty, I can give you as many as you like; would that be ok?" I say.

"My wife is parched, she's been praying all morning," Curly adds.

"No, I'm not thirsty. I just want to use the bottle to hang my *sheitel*!" Wiggy points out.

I go and fetch her a bottle of water, but when I come back, she is completely bald.

"Could you get my kosher turban from the overhead locker?" Wiggy asks.

I put the bottle down on the table, open the overhead locker and get her kosher headgear.

"One last favour. Do you mind hanging my *sheitel* on the bottle?" Wiggy begs.

"*Sheitel?*" I enquire.

"Yes, sorry, my wig," she explains.

"I've never done it before. Could you show me?" I ask her.

A hairy kind of experience…

Five minutes later, her tray table has morphed into a Jewish paraphernalia shop: a small menorah, a black bob hanging on a bottle of water, her husband's *teffilin* (a sort of tiny black transformer used for morning prayers), a Torah, a Nevi'm, and a Ketuvim *(Judaism's holy book triad)*.

I go and check the toilets; on my way back, passengers throughout the cabin, who have observed the whole incident, bombard me with questions.

"Is it real hair?"

"Is it fake?"

"What does it feel like?

"What's kosher hair?"

"Is she shaven all over?" the most indiscrete ask.

HOW AM I SUPPOSED TO KNOW THE ANSWERS TO ALL THESE QUESTIONS?

Just ask smartass, snoopy Mr Google Knowitall!

32

La Pilule

In the dead of night, while the whole of Africa is resting and Cape Town is still very far away, the lion does not want to sleep tonight, *awimmawe!*

"There's a passenger to move from 12A to 13B, can you deal with it?" my colleague asks me. "It's that lady travelling with her husband and two grandchildren."

One of those sweet couples of grandparents of advanced pensionable age taking the offspring of their upwardly mobile professional children around the world. Why on earth would the lady like to be moved now?

"She asked me for a tablet, she's got a headache," continues my colleague, "but since my French is pretty basic and rusty, I am not entirely sure why she wants to be moved. I think she might have had a domestic with her husband; could you try and talk to her since you can speak all those languages?"

And with this predicament of foreign languages, off I go to the passenger to organise her removal... Meanwhile, the lady presses the button to raise the divider between the two Business Class seats.

"You should watch it too, it would relax you; the children are asleep," he suggests while lowering the divider and ogling her.

"Enough!" she exclaims. "I am not up for any hippity-dippity. I have a splitting headache and it won't go away just by watching those things."

I don't really understand what I should do. In the dark, I wait, listen, and reflect. Should I move the wife of a grandfather playing with himself enjoying a dirty movie that he, however, kindly invited her to watch, or should I urge the octogenarian *monsieur* to lift his hands and stop immediately? Which action would inflict the least damage?

"I'm the one who's had enough!" the horny grandpa rants.

"If that's what you want, I'll move myself to another seat, so you'll have two empty seats next to you; let's see if you have any joy with your migraine!" On that note, he gets up with his crooked trousers, holding tight onto the zip with one hand and the computer with the other, the film still running.

His wife, free but visibly embarrassed, asks me, "*Une pilule, s'il vous plait, une pilule tout de suite.*"

What pill? I have a feeling he might have already taken the blue one. You're left with the red I am afraid, *Madame*!

33

Guile Beats Insulin!

...Hindu meal for 29K, Muslim meal for 31J, low sodium for 34A; I go back to the galley, draw the curtain, and try to relax for five minutes: all the 48 special meals are served!

"If this is a meal..." declares with a 'Primolevian' tone a passenger peeking through the curtain which should never be trespassed!

"Well," I answer sympathetically, "it's a diabetic meal as per your request." True, it looks like a rejected hospital meal, but when you order a medical meal you can't expect a Gordon Ramsey's presentation, can you?

"There we go again! I knew it, my wife has ordered a diabetic meal again! First of all, she hasn't got a clue how to deal with my illness. She doesn't know when I'm hypoglycaemic or hyperglycaemic; she follows me around with insulin. But today, I'll show you that I can beat my diabetes without insulin. Today I won't get my insulin fix!"

Last time I tried to argue with a diabetic I got slapped, so I'll do whatever he asks me. "If you prefer, I have a few regular meals left."

"Of course, give me at least two; I can't possibly have this phantom meal! Later, I'll explain my technique to you."

I kindly oblige.

Meanwhile, his tray table turns into a make-up artist's desk: jars of jam, mustard, sweet and savoury sauces, plus black, green, and pink pepper as well as a yogurt tub.

"The trick is to fool your body!" he tells me. "Leave everything on the table and take away this diabetic thingy! Even her, she wouldn't eat it," he says indicating the old Cantonese granny sitting next to him. First, he pushes it towards her and then pulls it. "See... what did I tell you?"

Yes, I can see. She is very hungry as well; but since I can't speak Cantonese, how can I explain to her that first you pretend to offer it to her and then you take it away? But let's focus on diabetes: our medical trainers tell us that diabetics can be aggressive or lethargic, pale or flushed, pissers or holders depending on whether it is hyper or hypoglycaemia. A real quagmire! A symptom minefield, really!

"And now I'll show you how to trick diabetes!"

He starts with a layer of brown sauce on a waffle, some apricot jam on bacon, blueberry yogurt on tomatoes, a spray of balsamic vinegar, a sprinkle of salt and pepper and he gulps down every last crumb in no time. "You must take it by surprise! Now, how can your body know if it needs sugars, fats or proteins, you tell me! This is how I avoid insulin; I told you, I'M NOT AN INSULIN ADDICT!"

I can't stop thinking that he might be addicted to something else, but I haven't got time to find out. The oversize English gentleman reclines his seat and falls in a deep sleep.

The Cantonese granny, with the clarity of her nine-tone mother tongue, tries to tell me something. Clear as mud. I'll have to interpret her gesticulation. From her rotating gesture, I gather she wants something to clean up the diabetic ogre's mouth. I get her some tissues straight away; volunteers are very rare these days. While she's cleaning him up, maybe she could no longer stand that awful view, he mutters something unintelligible along the lines of 'I haven't passed out… I'm just sleeping. I'm exhausted and slightly diabetic, but just a touch.'

Landed in Hong Kong.

"Bye Bye… See you… Cheerio…"

Disembarkations often feel endless and tiresome but occasionally a passenger shares a few words of wisdom…

"Did you see how I tricked my diabetes?! Don't become an insulin addict. You just need the right food combination!"

My mouth is already watering. Can't wait to become diabetic!

34

Wild Beasts

Ebola here, Ebola there, Ebola everywhere!

Everybody talks about Ebola on board these days! Cheer up and you'll get over it.

The galley panel displays an amber light. That means it's neither the interphone nor the passenger call bell, so what is it? Oh, yeah! It's somebody in the toilet, the usual kid playing with the buttons they should not be pressing. Good, I park the trolley, put the brake on and head for Toilet N at the back of the cabin; I join my hands in the praying position and become a father confessor for the day.

"How can I help you, my dear?"

"Yes, I know how to open the door; I am not stuck inside, I am also wearing my sari that protects me from any eventuality, but I think I have already been stung. It's huge, multi-legged, and hairy. The bug-eyed creature has a stinger that resembles a dipstick. I fear it's hiding behind the baby changing table."

The usual Three Hail Marys won't do the trick today, it's a more complex scenario; I should think of a more appropriate penance. Perhaps I should involve an entomologist. The lady is hitting and probably missing the beast on the walls; it sounds like a fight to the death. She appears pretty much au fait with martial art techniques, but I can't just leave her unarmed, I must offer a little help.

"Madam, I'm going to crack open the door from the outside, then…"

"No, don't you dare, it could sting the whole aircraft! And now that I think about it, this plane comes from Australia, it could be a flying fox… with Ebola around and all the rest of it… it could be mass extinction!"

From a bug to a flying fox in 2 minutes flat. What might the lady actually be seeing?

"Madam, could you just open it a little so that I can spray a very strong insecticide that we normally use in countries hit by malaria? Whatever it is, it won't stand a chance with this."

"Alright then, but be careful, though, it's very smart!"

I unbolt the door and spray the first can of deodorant that I can find in the galley. "Done, madam, now we'll wait for the legal two minutes. I am sure it will work."

Splash! Three flushes that would suck in even a dinosaur.

"Everything is fine now, I managed to suck it out of the plane. I can confirm it was a flying fox."

"Alright, madam, you can come out now, so we can treat the sting."

"Thanks," she says visibly dishevelled, with a Sai Baba-style hairdo and a big bump on her forehead.

"See here?"

"Yes, that's a huge bulge."

"I know why I was stung and what that means, tomorrow I have to attend a wedding, but that's a long story… It's ok, I wouldn't have let it sting any other passenger, though, we all have to accept our karma."

Indeed, I just wonder what stage I am at with mine.

We are definitely spiralling down.

Some time later.

"Nothing for me, thanks. All I need is a banana, if it's not too much trouble," a passenger asks me with her head cupped in her hands.

It would be a lot easier if I said 'no', but it sounds urgent, so I rush to the Business plantation to fetch one for her.

"Here you are, madam."

"Thank you!"

She grabs it, peels it and devours half of it in just one gulp.

"Fab!" she tells me stretching her fingers. "Potassium… it's instant." She carries on typing and then she looks at me, happy. "You know, I am a writer… I had a block."

I thought writer's block was a mental disorder, silly me!

"Potassium works immediately, my fingers were stuck, but I've now managed to finish the chapter.

And he kissed her on the cheek.

Then he hopped out of the room like a kangaroo.

I don't know what it sounds like in your language, but in English it's a powerful twist, I had to write it, it was buzzing around my head, you know. I could have written 'jumping with joy', but I chose a more creative, more original, and ultimately more romantic expression."

I must look for something to do, I have a feeling she's about to ask for my opinion.

"Do you know how I am going to title the book?"

The banana is working wonders; she's on a roll!

"I will love you tomorrow."

Born for the Pulitzer.

"Because she does not succumb to his charm easily, but then, she has a fatal accident, but readers don't know about that yet, and before expiring she tells him, 'I will love you...' and he imagines she tells him, 'forever', but she turns around and whispers, 'tomorrow', and then she dies. Do you like it?"

I had it coming.

I want to work in the hold… and no bananas.

35

An Apple a Day…

"Coleslaw?"

"What?" I just don't get it.

Mario and I are at the boarding door. A beautiful blond lady has just made an entrance with her two children on tow. Mario hands over the boarding card and mimes at me to take her to her seat in First Class with an undecipherable lip movement. I only catch the tail of it, it ends with an 'ow', it vaguely sounds like 'Coleslaw'. Is he trying to tell me at the wrong moment that when we land that's what he wants to order at the restaurant? I peruse the boarding card, the surname reads Martin, I look at her face, but I can't put two and two together. Mario, whose mouth is getting louder than usual, carries on with his secret lip code with passengers queuing up at the door. One of them, with an admirable spirit of solidarity, takes out an iPad and turns the screen towards me. One of those signs in large print that you normally see at arrivals in any airport around the world. Ok, it's taken me a while but at last I put Humpty Dumpty together. The blonde lady that I must take to First is no cabbage, it's Gwyneth!

Good, I show her to the front of the plane and on my way over I'm trying to think about all the articles that I've recently read about her. Is she married, divorced, re-married or single? The thing is… she's got two children with her…

In practice, my problem is the following: should I call her Mrs or Miss Paltrow? I try to recall all the articles in *Stop* magazine that I read when I go and visit my mum in Italy, gossip is a very serious business over there. Yes, I'll take another wild guess, since she's not a spring chicken anymore I'll go for an elegant... "Mrs Paltrow, please follow me this way, is there anything else I can do for you?"

"Yes, please. If you just moved back, I'd be able to sort myself out. Perhaps I shall send for you later, should Apple or Moses need something."

Ok, perhaps she's tired, or annoyed, or a combination of both...or maybe she wanted to be called 'Miss'.

Never mind titles; how on earth did it occur to her to call her daughter Apple? When she is eighteen, heaven forbid, she could become Mrs Mackintosh or, worse still, someone may call her Sweetie Apple Pie?

But today I'm on top of it, I work in Business Class and soon I shall be on my break. I'm already holding tight to my fragrant pyjamas and I head for the tail of the plane. I brisk walk through Economy trying to make myself as invisible as humanly possible and I think aloud about my warm little bed. I see a man with a strange scaffolding around his face who is wildly slapping himself. Shall I keep calm and carry on?

"Could you bring me a bottle of water, please?" the passenger sat next to him asks me.

They got me! Forget about sleeping...

"Of course, is it for him?" I ask after looking at the massive tangle of electrodes and suction cups coupled with a diving mask featuring flashing lights all over the frame. I take heart. He's not wearing fins, but he keeps on beating himself up mercilessly, nonetheless.

"He's on a virtual tour, by now he should have reached the stage where a swarm of bees attack him, you know, a bit like in *The Hunger Games*, soon he should reach the swamp, if he survives, but he often can't pass this level… I can send him a message though, I'll ask him to have a drink, he seems pretty agitated."

To me, he looks extremely flushed, I have never seen anybody voluntarily hitting himself so fiercely.

"Now, look! He must have reached the swamp."

Actually, I might have guessed by the arm movement, perfect breaststroke!

"He can't swim, so he keeps his head out of water, that's why he keeps on getting stung, I must send him a message, I'll tell him to dive in."

"Well, do what you have to do, this is the water you asked for," I say and sneak off. I don't know whether I'll be able to sleep after witnessing this assisted self-harming act.

End of break.

I've dreamt of swarming off with the rest of the bees and instead here I am in Business Class serving breakfast. I approach 12G, lying in her flat seat, who had ordered a full English breakfast.

The she alligator cracks an eye open; she waits for me to clip open the tray table and then snaps, "Ah! You woke me up! Can't you read? Can't you see that I wrote down that I didn't want to be disturbed? You did disturb me, didn't you? And don't look at me as if I were Barbra Streisand. I do eat crustaceans, shell and all if I feel like it, but I do say my prayers and I don't mix meat with dairy. And by the way, didn't you know it is forbidden to look at a sleeping Jewish woman?"

"Sorry, madam, I was just bringing your breakfast, as you ordered," I try to explain showing her the card that she herself had filled in at the beginning of the flight.

"Well, well, well! And do you think it was I filling out that card? It was that sleeping walrus over there," she tells me pointing at Mr Goldsmith next to her. "At any rate, he always sleeps through the most difficult times; I wonder if he was sleep-walking even when he married me in the synagogue."

Very well, now we have another piece of the puzzle. He's her husband.

"I put my curlers on to get my hair nice and wavy and he sleeps. I put my braces on to straighten my teeth and he sleeps. I have my nails done, all different from each other, and he sleeps. HE SLEEPS, SLEEPS, HE ALWAYS SLEEPS! AND HE DOESN'T EVEN NEED SLEEPING TABLETS! I, instead, haven't slept a wink for years!"

I would kindly like to remind her that she has just accused me of having woken her up, but I give up on it. And on the echo of the word "EEP" she shuts herself in the toilet.

10 minutes later.

Ding, ding

The light in toilet H illuminates, it must be insomniac Mrs Goldsmith. Despite the fact she is a very special case, I knock on the door as per normal procedure. As soon as I retract the knuckles from the door, the snake snaps out of the toilet covering her ears.

"Ahhhhhhh! FLUSH THE TOILET, PLEASE! FLUSH IT, I CAN'T! THAT BLOODY NOISE TERRORISES ME!!!" she shouts running down the aisle and curling up under the duvet in her flat seat. She keeps on staring at me, encouraging me to go in the toilet and follow her instructions.

Well. Here I am, in front of a smelly wide-open toilet with a raving lunatic staring at me. She won't give up until I have done it.

What shall I do? Do I press the flush button and move on? Yes, let's have some peace at the touch of a button. After all, there's a lot worse out there. There's someone whose name will always be Apple, but probably that's just comparing apples with oranges.

36

Ursa Major

"I'll throw him out of the window if you don't behave!"

"Oh, no mummy! It's so cold outside. Please don't!"

Your crew will point out the emergency exits nearest to you: there are two exits at the rear of the cabin and two...

Oops-a-daisy! A polar bear weighting half a tonne flies into my arms accompanied by the furious roaring of a little girl.

"MUM! He can't fly! Go and bring him back!"

Taxiing out.

While securing the cabin for imminent take-off, I'm faced with a MAJOR problem: finding a space for the little girl's 'Great Bear'. I quickly open a few overhead lockers, nothing! Ouch! I think I might have displaced my left shoulder.

On a Lagos flight, bags are as heavy as lead. For your 'nostos', you must bring lots of gifts, the more the better!

I can't find a space for the bear! It's too big and he keeps looking at me with his little glassy eyes and his croissant smile. I'd love to slap him! But I need to be calm, collected, and determined!

Ding, ding, ding, ding

There we go, the aircraft starts accelerating and I should already be strapped in! I can't waste any more time on a bear that is heading for extinction anyway... I run towards my jump seat while the little girl looks at me as if I were a bear snatcher; in a hurry, I open the toilet door and throw him in! I sit down just a split second before nose-up. Mission accomplished.

Soon, we will be up in the air where normally everything is calmer and quieter... As I get to the galley, a call bell goes off; it's them, mother and daughter.

"Give us Bear back!" they order me.

I go and fetch him from the loo. As if by magic, he's still enthroned. He is much better behaved than the little girl. For the whole take off, he hasn't moved an inch! I take him back to his owner in all his whiteness.

I start the bar service; the little girl asks me for a bag of ice ignoring her mother's attempt to convince her otherwise.

"What are you going to do with it?" the mother asks.

"It's for Bear. He's hot. He wants to soak his bum!"

There we go with a duty-free bag full of ice.

She opens the bag, places Bear's behind on ice and carries on drinking her fruit juice, pleased as Punch. She even offers some juice to Bear. She then checks with him the temperature is alright. A full dialogue... Let's hope he's happy... the situation might become unBEARable otherwise.

We land in Lagos, the usual weather: 35 °C, 110% humidity. Empty cabin. I carry out my security checks and who do I find? BEAR, all wet, and the duty-free bag splattered on the floor! Why did that evil child abandon him? I feel sorry for him and pick him up. Perhaps it was unintentional, she genuinely forgot him. I walk through the entire airport with Bear under my arm till I reach the baggage carousel. There they are mother and daughter! I approach them thinking she'll be thrilled to be reunited with Bear. Instead, she starts screaming, "Mum, I don't want him!!! He's wet himself!"

I give up and go straight to the Bear Lost&Found Office.

37

The Omnipresent

"God Bless you, you and... you, you'd better watch out!"

And so, between a blessing on the right and what looks like the last rites on the left, a visibly upset Texan wearing a fluorescent yellow tracksuit comes on board. A stray Stabilo Boss accompanied by his luminous wife wearing a flame orange trouser suit and a metallic green rose beetle blouse.

The highlights of our day!

"Relax, John..." whispers his spouse. "Now, just sit down and read something to take your mind off it. Have you got your Puzzle book out yet?"

"Is everything alright?" I ask fully aware of my wishful thinking, but I already know that the two living flares don't look particularly promising.

"Hi! I am a professor of theology," he illuminates me. "Today, I won't have any problems. The last time I flew was in 1982 on an ultralight and we crash landed, saved by a miracle..."

"...Praised be the Lord! But perhaps there's no use in digging up again certain unique experiences," intervenes his divine wife trying to dismiss her husband's inappropriate comments.

"We've dressed up for the occasion, anyway. You might have the black box but we, in our shimmering attire, will be the first to be found... even in the middle of the Atlantic!" shouts from the top of his lungs the fearless Texan pastor, determined to defy the skies after an unperceived absence of 35 years, no less!

I convince myself that, for the common good, it might be a stroke of luck to have them on board and I envisage a potential helicopter hovering over us at sea with the day-after headlines reading *Rescued Thanks to Mrs Green Beetle and Mr Canary Flapping in the Ocean*.

Pushing back.

His shoulders are starting to slump, his eyes are slanting, that hangdog expression on his face is heart-breaking, his tone really miserable. His canine Texan twang turns into feeble chick chirping.

"I'm paralysed..." he bleats to his wife who, with her *Pulp Fiction* jet black bob, mole glasses, red-hot lipstick, and a resolution worthy of a priest's housekeeper, has already struck her mental balance by staring at the void in front of her. And I think I am sitting right at the centre of that circular mental target, on my crew seat, ready to take off.

100 points.

"Do as I do, sleep!" she orders him with her eyes wide open.

"I just can't... I'm not having as much luck as you, I can't sleep with my eyes peeled like yours! Give me a pill, do something, for God's sake!"

"Knock it off and look straight ahead!" she adds dryly.

"Let's put it this way. I don't find it easy; the flight attendants are making me nervous. It's all a big pretence, they are paid to lie-smile!"

The lady, transfixed as if in cosmic meditation, cracks a smile at me. Is she still asleep, perhaps?

"I am scared stiff, Mary."

"Come on, that's enough!" she says turning her head towards her husband, who has now curled up as a hedgehog.

"Look at me when I talk!" she orders.

"Ahhh!"

I read the terror on his face and I empathise.

With that fierce glare that nearly split him in two, she can't expect him to calm down just by looking at her. And with that circular saw expression, you can't ask him to turn around. Actually, you are making my job almost impossible. How are we supposed to go all the way to London like this? Couldn't you try and pretend to be slightly less edgy?

As soon as we reach cruising altitude, I spring into action.

"It's not going to be this turbulent for the whole flight, you'll see that when we are above the clouds the aircraft will stabilize."

"How long have you been flying? I want to speak to the captain."

It's going to be one of those nights.

I tell my cabin manager about the case of the wandering Texan pastor. We decide to keep him under observation. And what about his wife? The woman, for all intents and purposes, is self-sufficient. He claims that she has no problems whatsoever and that she is having the time of her life. For what we can see, the situation is *Stabilo*: staring ahead, handbag on her lap firmly clutched by the handle with both hands, legs religiously together and clenched lips. Never seen such stiffness before, not even at Madame Tussauds'.

"She's asleep, can't you see?" he assures us. "She can relax (?), but I can't!"

If things carry on like this, we shall have to cancel the meal service.

We decide to call the captain, sometimes it works.

"...The pressure exerted by air on all bodies at all times in all directions is called air pressure. When air..." the captain explains to the pastor who, by the looks of it, does no longer know which patron saint to pray to. Today we have a far too technical and not very empathic captain. It doesn't work. We think we might have to phone MedLink, our doctors on the ground that from Arizona have a quick fix for every ache.

"I know how to handle this!" exclaims my Togolese colleague. "Our Lord is everywhere, John. The Almighty is here with us even now, can you feel it?"

"Yes," he replies staring at the floor. "Please, carry on. I'm usually the one preaching, but today I'm very happy to play second fiddle."

"Look out of the window and reach out for his hands, can you see them? One over here…" and our colleague encourages us to look outside and confirm.

"Yes!" we all fib in unison.

"Uhm…" he utters not so convinced but hopeful.

"And the other is over there," she says indicating the window on the opposite side.

We all turn around pointing in that direction.

"Yes, he is over here," we all blatantly lie and meanwhile we take him to safety in the galley, immediately transformed into a makeshift sacristy waiting for a miracle to happen.

"We are safe, we are protected, God is everywhere!" proclaims Christelle. "And now let's hold each other's hands and let's pray."

We make a circle and our colleague recites words that only a pastor's daughter could know.

"Spirit of the living God, present with us now, protect and support us from up above."

"Sky Almighty, are you opening a portal?" asks a passenger who's just got into the galley. "It's good that you're doing it here, in no man's land, at home it can be dangerous, and if there isn't an expert conveyor who's able to close it… can I join you?"

John calms down, his wife keeps on travelling asleep in an advanced state of *rigor mortis* with her eyes wide open, we are

connected with the spiritual world in a celestial Ring a Ring-o'
Roses...

Are we nearly falling down or what?

38

Silurian Love

A curled index finger calling you is never a harbinger of good news.

"Pssst, pssst… Come closer, I must whisper something in your ear."

To be honest, my head is still inside the toilet for the routine checks (messages on the mirror written with a lipstick by the odd rogue, smoke detectors that might have been tampered with), but given her persistence, I put everything on hold.

"I'm scared."

Pause.

I move my ear away from her mouth and stare at her.

Definitely frightened.

She opens and closes the window blinds, once, twice, three times.

"Did you see it?"

Despite my best intentions, I wouldn't have time to see anything at that speed.

"No, I'm not sure I have seen it, could you re-open it, please?"

"Yes, but only for a split second, otherwise they spot us."

The Aussie woman fully opens the blind and turns around towards me.

"Look, go on! Look and tell me that something can be done about it."

I concentrate on constellations, no sign of turbulence whatsoever, not one cloud as far as the eye can see; I just can't think of what I should be seeing and since I don't want to hurt anyone's feelings, I kindly ask her at least to point at where I should be looking.

"Over there, somebody's following us, someone's flying next to us…"

"Ah!" I exclaim with all the empathy I'm capable of.

Mission failed.

"See, I knew it! You don't believe me either; you're all the same, you cabin crew, you never take seriously enough what you're told. You always smile, but then…"

Look who's talking, with that bouncy feathered hair and all those braids perfectly huddled one next to each other hanging over her straight shoulders. A real trichological chairoplane. Is she taking me for a ride?

"Honestly, I don't know what you're talking about, please explain."

"Uniform. Foxtrot. Oscar. U.F.O. There's not much to explain."

She drags me to the aft door explaining that from there it'll be easier to spot the spaceship following us and that she'll be able to tell what they're up to by the shape of their vessel.

I run through my mind all the episodes of *Sapphire & Steel*, all the speeches by Stephen Hawking, but to no avail. This is *Space: 1999* material.

The interphone rings, it's the captain for the usual checks.

"See, even they realized it, didn't they? It's the captain... You'd better tell me the truth..." and she snatches the handset out of my hand. "Captain? Jupiter has just left Gemini and is now in Cancer, I have no time to explain everything now but, in a nutshell, there's a spaceship following us, you can see it better from the back of the plane," and she hangs up.

A few minutes later the captain arrives to talk to the Aussie.

"Sky Almighty! Show me where the spaceship is."

"There."

I'm rather curious to see what *he* can see. At least I was able to utter 'Ah!' to her. The captain is getting closer and closer to the door but is quite unable to take his eyes off... some not so celestial aspects. He smirks at her, which is worrying, but he does not look worried in the least.

"There! But there's no point if you don't want to see it... I was exactly the same when I used to be a hairdresser at The Rocks. I didn't want to believe many things, but since I became a professional astrologer, I have relaxed and opened my eyes. Now the world appears for what it actually is. There is a crack in the fabric of time. That's where they come in from."

Too many seasons of *Doctor Who*…

The captain listens and above all enjoys the view from top to bottom, lingering on more than one part. With earthly interest, he asks her whether he can visit her studio in Sydney; he encourages her to go back to her seat promising that he'll do his best to change path.

I'm no longer sure I have chosen the right career…

"Maggie, now I have to go back to the flight deck. After all, someone has to fly this plane. I'll make them eat our dust, our stardust, Maggie!"

She is ecstatic and can't stop twirling her hair.

"Alright, captain, I look forward to the appointment in my studio."

He walks back, turning around every now and then; she waves at him with a giggle, he turns around again, she winks at him, he trips over a seat, she sniggers, he chuckles.

Pathetic.

I thought every aircraft had that flashing light on the tip of the wing.

"Franco, did you realise that the captain is a Silurian? They're the nicest."

39

To Board or Not to Board, This Is the Question

A violent thunderstorm is battering Toronto. Will our crew manage to get on board safe and sound?

On the airport-bound coach.

Doomsday sky, *Watch Tower* style. The Great Flood has begun. I'm dreaming of a canoe; I can paddle better than Pocahontas! Simply by looking out of the window, empowered with the gift of omniscience, our pilots proclaim that the airport has been hit by lightning at least twice. Some of my colleagues, in denial, draw the curtain, they don't want to know; they just pray to reach the 767 that will fly us back to the Land of Albion.

Pilots cannot accept the ineluctability of the Great Flood. Their isobar brains seem to be able to influence both weather and time.

"Drive, when did you last replace your windscreen wipers?"

"It's not a question of wipers; I carry on just because I know this road by heart."

"Do you know it well?"

"I take you to and fro the airport three times a day."

"Are the headlights working properly?"

"No idea... but I'm already in amphibian mode, there is nothing more I can do!" he offers jokingly to defuse tension. "Just relax, you'll soon be in the air, and perhaps up there, in your element, you'll feel safe..."

We get to the airport by the skin of our teeth; the dispatcher breaks the tragic news: the whole area has been stricken by lightning at least three times. *Wow, our pilots really have the gift of clairvoyance!* Delays galore; we'll need to be very patient, luggage might have to be loaded manually. *Fantastic, there's time for a cup of coffee!*

At Starbucks', an endless queue of desperate people who, not knowing how long they'll have to wait, want to have a little treat of some sort... et voilà, TOTAL BLACKOUT in the entire airport!

What about our coffee?

People start getting nervous; all this darkness, in an otherwise shining and sparkling world, isn't normal. Outside, thunder and lightning; inside, deafening silence. People grope in the dark looking for each other, some cry, others indulge in petty theft for the inconvenience suffered.

"A KNIFE HAS BEEN FOUND IN A BAG!" shouts a woman turning towards the Starbucks' queue while fleeing.

"Oh my god!!! How long is the blade?" asks the queue in unison.

"I don't know!" the woman answers without slowing down. "At least 20 inches! Run!"

A veiled woman (with no knee pads, OUCH!) crawls on her knees in front of the Starbucks patrons and lifts her arms into the air in a praying fashion. For some very strange reason, she feels the need to explain herself, "I've been working in this airport for the past 16 years (*Jupiter Tonans probably doesn't care...*), and there's never been a blackout before. Even the emergency lights aren't working!!! Oh good Lord, what will become of us?"

The queue remains silent, they don't know what to say and, in all likelihood, they don't appreciate that 'us'. Zeus seems to pay no attention to the supplicant and keeps thunderbolting away. But what can really happen to 'us'? We all need to calm down. A decaffeinated tea, perhaps? Some start panicking while others give in to catalepsy. In the waiting area for the Moscow flight, a violin begins to play in the dark, immediately accompanied by another nearby.

Please, let's not conjure up a Titanic atmosphere!

The end is near.

A guitar follows suit... the bow could tilt at any time and the airport might sink into Lake Ontario, crashing Leonardo and his figurehead!

"Ahhhhhh! Apparently, it has a retractable blade! But don't buy into it, it'll be Halloween soon!" shouts a man running in the opposite direction. "The guy could be hiding anywhere; rumour has it he's gone into the ladies'! Also, did you hear that a fireman died while trying to put out a fire?"

A sinking boat-airport, Russian violins playing to the very end, a veiled woman praying to God only knows what God, the crowd groping in the dark, a mysterious passenger carrying a retractable blade knife... A feeling of impending doom is fast spreading through the airport.

Then, electricity miraculously comes back.

Fiat lux et lux facta est.

End of the doom and gloom.

The dispatcher calls the crew to the boarding door. "Come on guys, get onboard, an airplane is the safest place in a thunderstorm."

I enter the jetty and 'bladerun' to safety!

40

Vitamin K of a Different Kind

"This time I'll answer it, but the next is all yours," I declare matronly to my colleague Paul who, having seen where the call bell comes from, tries to flee the scene.

Truth be told, the outfit is rather disturbing. I get close to Mr McCoy who, for the last hour or so, has been wearing his night 'harness': a sort of grey foam hot-air balloon dominating the whole cabin, with a tiny slot for his mouth, two small holes for his nose and two slits for his eyes from where, I reckon, he can catch a glimpse of reality as we know it. When I ask him what that 'idiosoma' is, he tells me it is a kind of protective helmet that he wears to calm down…

"I'd like a bottle of water, preferably with a spout, it's easier to drink."

"I only have a spout-less bottle of water, would that be alright? You can take your helmet off to drink it and then put it back on."

Am I really talking to a human tick?

"Just get me a straw then. On a plane? At night? Take off my helmet? You must be joking; I wouldn't feel safe! Not a chance!"

It sounds like a sensible answer… for a psychiatric ward…

Ding! The 'FASTEN YOUR SEATBELT' sign comes on.

I walk through Business Class to check passengers in, making sure they are all sitting down with their seatbelts fastened. I spot some empty seats, nothing to worry about. On a flat-bed seat by the window, I notice two movements: a succussatory one to the South and a spasmodic-undulatory one to the North.

Interesting, but what about the seatbelt?

I lift up the duvet. Surprise, surprise! I discover not one, but two... active individuals, in a revolutionary post-1968 position, who look at me like two moles who haven't seen daylight for quite a while. Feeling observed, they clumsily try to factor back to a more presentable numeric combination. The girl goes back to her seat; "Anyway, it's all that guy's fault, he's been selling Vitamin K in front of the Economy toilet," she says half embarrassed and half annoyed, with a hint of a Nordic accent.

Economy toilet? A philander selling Vitamin K? *Back in my day, you would buy it at a chemist's.* I turn round and see a man with a white suit talking to two visibly overexcited and dreamy girls. What's going on? Should I really believe two people who, when caught in the Gemini position, swore they ended up like that because of a drug dealer who has set up shop in front of the Economy toilet and is now luring two more customers with his... Vitamin K?

"I think we should get the police involved," suggests Christine, my upright colleague.

"Look Christine, soon we'll be in San Fran; it's Halloween... Why don't we go to the Castro and forget about it? Will the police ever believe the report of two crew members who have been talking to a human tick and caught in the act two aroused moles and a Vitamin K pusher doing Business in Economy? What happens in the air, stays in the air. Live and let them take their Vitamin K supplements!"

41

Drawing a Merciful Veil

"An apple juice."

"I beg your pardon?"

"AN APPLE JUICE!!!"

Oh my God, I'm really deaf today, I can't hear what they say. The problem is that you get used to the noise and then everything seems normal; but for how many hours has the little girl been shouting on the other aisle? I hope she won't carry on for the whole flight to Doha! Saint Qatarine, *ora pro nobis!*

Instead of being gagging for drinks, passengers are begging for any kind of ear plugs, but our supplies have long gone! A non-head-to-toe veiled woman has asked to be moved to the other aisle because she couldn't hear herself think, let alone concentrate on the Quran. She cocoons up with onboard blankets. Inside her makeshift chrysalis she manages to find some much-coveted peace and quiet and can carry on reading her surahs, trying to find a prayer that might placate the *infanta*.

The burka-wearing mother is not worried. As calm as a Hindu cow, she slaps her, she smacks her, she hits her but to no avail; the girl doesn't stop howling at her mother's abaya. Three Wise Men come from Business Class bearing some sort of gifts to try and tame her, but the wild child doesn't want to know and sends them back.

This time, myrrh does not do the trick.

"My daughter would like a whole row so she can throw herself on the seats and bang her tummy."

"As you can see, the flight is not very busy, so that wouldn't be a problem at all. But what do you mean exactly by 'throw herself' and 'bang her tummy'?"

"Well, that's what she does at home on the sofa. She stands on the armrest, throws herself, bounces back a few times and then relaxes."

If this is the price of peace…

"Please, go ahead. But I've said and seen nothing!"

Will it work? I go back to the galley, but I keep an eye on the whole throwing-bouncing operation. The little girl really plunges on the seats tummy down while shouting something like 'oooooOOOOOOOooooo' and back she bounces… scores of times! By now, she should be all black and blue and completely stunned. Buckles and edges should have worked wonders!

I step in, I think that's enough battering for a day, the aim is not to get her killed. In the meantime, a fully veiled lady intervenes and is now arguing with the mother. The two black panthers are having a heated debate in the dark, a fierce veil to veil. I'm also in the dark, I don't understand a word of what is being said, I struggle to make out who is who. I ask a nearby gentleman to help me with a sort of concise translation of the animated exchange. "They are both travelling in the same direction while taking different paths. (*They don't sound that philosophical to me*) In essence, one doesn't agree with the other: the lady on the left says that the mother is raising her daughter as a boy and argues that's the reason why the little girl is so angry and upset," he tells me.

Some food for thought, I will ponder on male children farming... but more importantly, will the possessed missy calm down?

Passengers are getting ever more restless and hopeless; some adopt a 'Stevie Wonder' position, rocking in desperation with their headphones at full blast; some pray to Allah the Merciful, asking for some miracle and while waving their arms in the air and feeling sorry for themselves, they say "Why us, why us??? Inshallah!"

For all the camels of Rajasthan! In the whole history of aviation, no landing has ever been so welcomed. The last people to get off are obviously the howler's parents. She's asking to be dragged through the cabin like a rag doll or else... The mother pulls her through the aisle by a leg and asks the father to make sure her hair doesn't get dirty... what about the rest???

Once they get to the door, it's the father's turn. The little girl wants to put her knees around his neck and hang down on his back, with her hair touching the floor, while they get down the stairs. What was the point in 'making sure her hair doesn't get dirty'? At last, they get on the bus taking them to the terminal.

I'm also terminal and I need to get my eardrums checked!

42

Barbara-Ann

"Don't worry, just place them sideways, they will both fit. I'll go in the middle, you two help me on either side of the overhead locker. On the count of three, push!"

"But you… are you Barbara-Ann?" the girl on my left asks the Valkyrie that has just arrived and looks ever so determined to shove her XXXL bag in the locker too.

"Yes, I am Barbara-Ann."

Meanwhile, I stay put in the middle in the receiving position of a professional weightlifter waiting for the two to recognize one another and lay their precious valuables at last.

"OMG! Am I dreaming or what? Are you really Barbara… Barbara-Ann?" the fan shouts jumping up and down for joy with both feet.

"Shall we close it?" I say glaring at both. "I think we have established that the lady is Barbara-Ann but if you carry on jumping like that, you'll wake up Mrs Pembroke's Labradors! She's travelling in First Class and she was assured that in the hold no stroboscopic lights are used; her dogs are epileptic, you know."

As I share that essential information, in the back of my mind I flick through every single issue of *Hello* magazine. Not even the shadow of someone by the name of Barbara-Ann appears on the horizon; who the heck might she be? The name doesn't ring a bell.

"Yes, we can shut," replies the ecstatic girl still in disbelief that Barbara-Ann is really on board.

"Aw, Barbara-Ann, where are you sitting, Barbara-Ann? Is it really you, Barbara-Ann?"

If she repeats that name once again, I'm going to have to strangle her. True, we're used to pretty much anything, Hanna & Barbera, Santa Barbara, Conan the Barbarian, but what on earth got into her mother when she decided to call her Barbara-Ann? What was wrong with just calling her Barbara, or even Ann for that matter? Sometimes, even the best ingredients, in the wrong combination, turn out to be a disaster. What's this Barbara-Ann? An ode to onomastic indecisiveness?

The 'diva' sits down, and I can't resist whispering a question to the overexcited girl, "But, between you and I, who is Barbara-Ann?"

"Crickey! Don't you know? What planet do you live on? She is the world-famous yoga teacher from Vancouver, some sort of meditation guru; people come from the four corners of the globe to see her!"

I can't believe my luck, I have the honour of having her on board, in my cabin, Barbara-Ann, no less, who incidentally is sitting by the window into the abyss of Economy Class.

"Chicken curry or pesto pasta?" I ask the Indian lady sat with her daughter next to the unrivalled Barbara-Ann, currently in cosmic meditation and in the lotus pose (I am not experienced enough to ascertain whether it's open or closed, it looks pretty much withered to me).

"For me, pesto pasta and for my daughter too; what about the lady, is she not eating?"

"No," I say, "Don't you know that when Barbara-Ann meditates she doesn't eat for days?"

Four rows ahead, I ask Barbara-Ann's disciple the same question, which is not that tricky, actually it's the same for everybody from nose to tail. "Chicken or pasta?"

"What did Barbara-Ann have?" asks the fanatic while standing up and pointing at her in the grip of an irrepressible impulse.

"Barbara-Ann decided to fast because she's meditating. Would you like to follow her example?"

"Absolutely! Barbara-Ann is so good! And did she drink?"

"No," I assure her, "when she meditates, she dry fasts."

I think the crazed devotee should now be sorted; the tail of the plane is getting closer. Good. I start clearing in the trays and I recapture Barbara-Ann in the same lotus pose with a broccoli floret on her knee, a carrot between her fingers and a gherkin on her thigh. I find this Arcimboldo-style scene quite fascinating. The Indian child, the only survivor in her row, tells me under her breath, "Have you noticed that Barbara-Ann is fast asleep? I did ask her to play with me, but she preferred to sleep in this cross-legged position, so I started throwing vegetables at her, it serves her right! Vegetables are disgusting anyway; besides, she won't know it was me. So, where can I put the boiled spud?"

43

Hourly Possession

"Ladies and Gentlemen, duty free! Any Duty free? Gift items, cigarettes, alcohol? Duty free. Just remember, Christmas is fast approaching, don't get caught out! What's the point of Boxing Day if you ain't got any boxes to throw away? Duty free?" I shout peddler-style while walking through the cabin pushing the duty-free trolley and waving our inflight brochure.

"Oh yes! Finally! Absolutely, yes! Please!"

Oh my God, I've never seen anyone so enthusiastic about duty free!

"Well, I'd like… I'm so excited! I'd like to buy the Philips projector! Oh, look, my hands are shaking in anticipation!"

"Yes, just let me check if I have it." I open a couple of drawers and manage to find it. "Here we go, there it is!" I say while handing over the coveted item to the passenger.

"So, this is it. Am I really holding it in my hands?"

"Yes, Sir. That's the projector you asked for."

"Don't you find it amazing? The best things do come in small packages…"

Not knowing what we are talking about, and not only completely ignoring its usefulness but even its existence, I decide to go for a generic and multipurpose, "Lovely!"

He gets his wallet out, gives me his card, and with a swipe, I charge him £400 for something the size of a pen.

3 hours later…

The projector man comes to the galley trying not to draw any attention to himself or the little bag he is carrying and whispers to me, "The lady next to me is fast asleep, I'd like to return the wonderful item you sold me earlier on. I knew from the very beginning that I didn't really need it… but it was nice to own it just for a few hours. I feel so content, it was a dream come true. Even the lady next door was ecstatic for me, I don't want to disappoint her. And did you notice the way the man across the aisle was looking at me? Green with envy he was! It felt so good! So please, let's be very discreet… I'd like to be refunded. I know you also feel sorry for me, but I can't really afford this magnificent piece of technology. But the thought of having held it in my hands for a couple of hours as if it were mine… look, it still gives me goosebumps! But don't worry, one day I will buy it, I promise…"

True, a promise is a promise… but if I were you, I would spend £400 to see a good non-returnable shrink!

44

Works of Bodily Mercy

"That way, please. Your seat is on the other aisle. Lovely hat, by the way."

"Thanks, I think it makes me glow, doesn't it? Shame I should always walk around with this moth at my heels," whispers the lady at the boarding door.

"Uhm..." hesitates her husband slightly embarrassed, clearing his voice, "the aforementioned lepidopteron would be me, as it happens. My wife is a clown, she's always up for a laugh... she calls me that because I love flying!"

"No, Graham, I went way out of my way; I could have called you a crab for that matter. Any chance of downgrading him to Economy at all?" begs Mrs Wright.

Wow! That would be one of those extremely rare cases of downgrading in the history of aviation, requested and granted on the spot. Tempting... but no, we haven't even left yet, let's get on with it, for God's sake! Patience, all things are difficult, before they become easy, as they say. Shall we carry on with boarding, yes or no? Slowly but surely, we are getting there. Today they are coming on in dribs and drabs.

"Then there's this lady called... can't even pronounce it," the dispatcher tells me breathless with the radio stuck to her ear. "Yes, I've got her here. I know, she is an Eyetie. No habla Ingles!

I'm 'bout to load her." By the terminology she uses, she must be a former cargo girl and she is definitely getting her Costas and Rivieras mixed up!

"No problem, I'll look after her," I say before one word too many slips out of her mouth.

"She has a slight limp," she whispers in my ear, "Naaah, I'm sure she's used to it; I reckon you can take the crutches off of her, plonk them in the wardrobe and let her walk to her seat in her own time. I betcha, she'll make a beeline for her chair. At the end of the day, I don't have all day, do I?"

"Signora Barellina, come with me, I'll take you to your seat, just hold on to my arm."

"Oh, what a wonderful Italian accent. Well, I wanted to clarify one thing…" And on the way to the seat, she bursts into laughter. "As I was saying, there are no clues in my surname. You and I know perfectly well that 'Barellina' means 'little stretcher' in our beautiful language, but I am not going to need a carrying bed today."

She keeps on marching to her own drum. I just want to take her to her seat and zoom back to the boarding door to help my colleague finish off with the rest of the passengers.

But the lady is still doubled over in laughter and shouts, "I have never laughed so much in my life, I am a pass(enger)ing crippled! I mean, it's all new to me as well; I certainly wasn't born one, I am not used to wheelchairs and crutches, I am afraid today it's going to be a very sticky business… ah ah ah!"

She is in stitches, she likes her own company, she staggers a bit and then falls on the floor, while a long queue of born-angry passengers builds up behind her. "I'm getting up now, don't be impatient. Franco, give me a hand, will you? Thank God, there's an Italian able-bodied on board today!"

Today is my lucky day, forget about winning the lottery.

I leave the transient limping passenger on her seat and rush back to the door, ready to welcome... crippled number 2!

"She's in 20J, could you take her as well while you are at it?"

Of course, I wasn't born Italian for nothing, Signora Barellina has just said it, right?

"Come with me, madam, do take my... other arm." Thank God I have got two. It would all be too much for just one.

We waddle all the way down to the back of Business Class and then I look at the lady's boarding card: 15A. Double trouble: wrong seat, wrong aisle.

"Madam, we have to walk back, I am afraid."

"Are you kidding me?"

"Catch her, catch her, she's about to pass out!" a passenger shouts.

I must admit it, as a kid I was never good as a goalkeeper. My intuition for the football direction has always been nothing to write home about. Which side will she fall on? Luckily, she is tiny, and she falls right into my arms like a dead leaf. Proud of myself and with my best Unhappy Prince face, I carry her to her seat but while I am in character, I will challenge somebody to a duel. No sooner do I make one step forward, than the air version of Madame Bovary is perfectly awake and demands I should also carry her bag.

What? Is it a pre-planned fainting?

"Good job!" exclaims the whole cabin wholeheartedly while the luckiest person on board is carrying the 19-th century crippled from one aisle to the next. I lay her down on her seat in a sweat and the disabled New Yorker gives me her shopping list.

"I want a magazine, a glass of champagne, a pink grapefruit juice and something to munch on. Then I must take my medications… and, by the way, is the Wi-Fi on yet?"

"No, madam, there's no Wi-Fi on board today, I am afraid."

"What? I have to phone my orthopaedist!"

"Is it that urgent?"

"Yes, I forgot to ask him whether my foot can cope with the cabin pressure; perhaps I'd better talk to the captain first, I need some technical details, I have more metal inside this leg than a bulldozer. My foot is a sort of improper weapon. Should it explode, it could be carnage, a cobalt bomb, a shrapnel, understood?"

By now, I have learned one thing: not all the disabled are equal. For instance, there's the accidental crippled, the explosive crippled and what else? Is it over for today?

After a hiccup boarding, at long last we are up in the sky where we belong.

"Ladies and Gentlemen, it's your cabin manager speaking. My name is George Michael and if there's anything I can do to make your flight more comfortable, please feel free to ask…"

Yeah, right, but after that name, the content of the message is totally irrelevant. Massive buzz on board.

"George Michael?!" a passenger sat opposite me asks glowingly.

In the cabin, a mini choir is humming its way to New York.

"Yes, it's him! Since he was caught red handed engaging in obscene acts in public, and it wasn't the first time, he has been given community service, that's why he is on board our flight," declares another passenger.

Really? I can't believe it… What? Is the lady insinuating I am in constant rehabilitation?

"Got you! (not really). Instead of acting like an old lecher around public toilets, they brought him on board to clean them. That makes sense," says her husband.

Ding, ding

The lady presses the call bell after touching up her make-up and combing her dishevelled hair.

I am not going. I'll send George Michael. I pick up the interphone and tell him that a passenger in 26A asked after him.

"Yes, madam, how can I help you?" Michael asks.

Had she seen the Grim Reaper, she'd have had more things to tell him. And yet his name badge on the lapel reads George Michael.

"Everything's fine, sorry to bother you."

Ah! Homonymy… cheeky bugger!

And this year, once again, at Christmas time, you broke another heart, Georgie!

♬ *Last Christmas, I gave you my heart,*

But the very next day, you gave it away ♬

45

Sisilia, Land of Lemons!

"Duty free?" Yippee! Today they almost ate me alive! I park my duty-free trolley and I get a bite to eat at last! Sat on my crew seat, I savour my Middle Eastern flavoured salad with the curtains strictly drawn to avoid swarms of passengers unexpectedly flying in. But the lure of the stage is irresistible.

Curtain!

"Aw! Che buono limoni de Sisilia!" (Sicilian lemons are really lovely!) peekaboos a Canadian passenger.

"Yes, indeed!" I confirm. But wasting time talking about Sicilian lemons with your mouth full is on the verge of being rude. I mean, you can have a citrusy conversation in the doctor's waiting room, in a car if and when you get stuck on the motorway and you're lucky enough to have company, but certainly not when you are enjoying one of the most sacred times of the day, lunch!

"Franco, is that right? I read your name on the badge on the lapel of your jacket, you certainly look Italian; whereabouts are you from?"

The insane desire to tell her that I am a fourth-generation Argentinian and that I only speak the Cymbrian language crosses my mind... but then a whole different saga would begin, too much to explain, too many mountains to talk about and everybody knows that too much of a good thing can spoil the broth, which, by the way is tasting delicious. I'd better let her vent in Italian, usually after a while they give up and leave. Advanced students of Italian are few and far between; they normally don't go beyond the gastronomic basics that allow them to ransack any Italian delicatessen in sight.

"Yes, I am Italian, we love to eat… (*in peace, perhaps?*)"

"Oh, *bene*! Take it easy, don't worry, whenever you can, I would like to show you a conversation on my computer. You know, lately I've been to Sicily and now I fully understand the profound meaning of *amore*! I can still smell those big lemons! *Che profumo di limoni!*"

"Actually, I couldn't agree more, in Sicily they have such delicious and fragrant lemons!"

Now, however fragrant lemons might be, my opinion is that they deserve no longer than a 5-minute chat, but between a bergamot and a tangerine, at least 15 minutes elapse and I should already be going for my break, but the point is still late arriving.

But sooner or later there is always a point.

"You know how sensitive and emotional us women are… I met a certain Salvatore. He doesn't speak English and I only speak Google Italian. Something happened between us… some kind of wordless communication, d'you get me?"

No, but I can very well imagine: speechless love!

"Since I don't know you from Adam, I am not in the least embarrassed in showing you our conversation, because, in my effort to speak Italian, I am not sure I explained myself very well;

it's been 15 days since he last wrote to me. I am pretty worried. Wouldn't you be?"

Devastated, actually.

"Right, I am on my break now, but I'm happy to help you. It seems pretty serious, I feel responsible."

Hence a conversation in Italian follows that more or less literally translated sounds like so.

Sue, it's Salvatore, here. But what do you want from me?

I don't want anything, only feeling something of you.

She keeps staring at me awaiting confirmation. "All I wanted to say was that I felt something inside for him and I looked it up on Google translator. Does that sound right in Italian?"

"Look, Sue, sometimes this Google Italian sounds a bit ambiguous. And you could have avoided the courtesy form. I know you wanted to impress him, but you already 'know' each other well enough, biblically speaking, to skip these formalities."

But who am I to stop their little games? Perhaps they find this formal way of talking enticing?

She shows me the screen once again.

I got you, Sue, you are a sentimental kind of 'zoccola'.

I can't wait to go back to Sicily to see you and hear you call me 'zoccola' time and time again.

And then she says, "I know that literally translated 'zoccola' means 'slut' but he means it figuratively, of course, otherwise he wouldn't have called me a 'sentimental zoccola', surely there's something between the lines that escapes me."

Even the illustrated alphabet is useless at the moment. I can't think of a figurative way for the word 'slut'.

Sue, be warned! The moment you set foot in Sicily, I'll Big Bang you crazy...

Sei molto dolce ed esplosivo. So che ti piaceva quando ero avvinghiata tutta intorno a te.

And here she asks me for a back translation into English of her Google Italian version.

You are very sweet and explosive. I know you liked it when I was wrapped all around you.

"But I didn't mean that; what I had on the tip of my tongue was that I enjoyed him being around me."

"Well, Sue, I see what you mean but that's not quite the way we say it in Italian; I am afraid he might take you for a non-figurative 'zoccola'. I'm only trying to preserve your reputation here."

Moving on.

I did notice that. If you want it, come back to Cefalù and don't keep me waiting.

"Franco, I am convinced he is very much in love and impatient, isn't he? What do you think I should do? There's a strong understanding between us as you can see."

Not a verbal one... yet.

"Should I keep on writing to him?"

Well, judging from the level of your communication, I think it doesn't make much of a difference, however... if you want to carry on using the courtesy form, please do, because respect comes first.

Ah! Che buono limoni de Sisilia!

46

Not by Tea and Coffee Alone

In the long nights when the jetlag keeps you awake and insomnia becomes your only friend, after watching all possible series, what do cabin crew do? They study… and then when they finally land back at base what do they do? They sit their exams! So not only are they beautiful/handsome, charming, nice, patient, and indestructible but also smart and cultured!

They are indeed a new species: *Homo Sapiens^2 Stewardensis*

"Those of you with a calculator, please write down the model number on the form in front of you," announces the fearsome Open University Invigilator.

What about us sitting our Classical Studies exam? We just need to know the entire *Iliad* and *Odyssey* by heart, as well as *The Persians* by Aeschylus, *Lysistrata* by Aristophanes, Pericles' *Funeral Oration* and all the rest… are we not allowed a 'dating machine' or a 'Homerometer' during the exam?

"This calculator's model is not allowed. I'll have to take it away, I'm afraid," states dogmatically the Invigilator.

Really, you can't speak like that, Invigilator! You are going to scare the life out of the poor thing. He might even faint and cause problems for all of us. Said and done. Open and close the window, do you think you are up to it? The Invigilator provides him with a calculator that to our mere mortal eyes looks exactly the same as the one she has just confiscated.

"3,2,1… you can turn your exam paper page now… Good luck to you all. You have three hours." Her tone is so terrifying that I forget why I'm here and for a split second I'm convinced I'm taking part in *The Hunger Games*. Is it better to head towards the cornucopia and get the best weapons or flee straight into the loo for a solitary surge of… before starting?

It's all coming back to me, I'm here for my exam!

"You, sitting A219 can only keep a pen, a pencil, and a rubber on your desk!"

But at least, are we allowed to go to the loo? Or do you need a calculator for that as well?

47

The Protocol

Zimbabwe, what a wonderful country! Fertile plains, savannah as far as the eye can see, massive watercourses, majestic wildlife, now all torn apart. Since the last time we came, things have changed dramatically. Harare, the capital city, is a ghost town. Like in many other African capitals, the vehicles that used to choke its streets are just a distant memory. The only automobiles around are government cars; people have no access to petrol, there's no gas for cooking and no food to put on the table. You can count people around on your fingertips, deafening silence; the atmosphere is that of a covert curfew.

The tragic situation has also affected our bubble, the five-star hotel where we stay is on its last legs. From London, we brought a few essentials that are immediately rationed amongst the staff. Our female colleagues, moved to pity by the desperation lingering in the air, have their nails and hair done every single day. Even us boys contribute to the local economy with corn and hair removal, but there is a limit to how much hair even the most hirsute can sacrifice to the cause.

Imire no more, our favourite animal sanctuary where we stayed a couple of years ago. I remember we had lunch by the lake while the elephants roamed around freely; an old herd matriarch shyly got nearer to us and, out of curiosity, stretched her trunk towards us for a brief yet intense contact. During the night, we were moved to tears by an extraordinary event: the birth of a white rhinoceros.

Today, with a few cans of kerosene, they manage to secure our safe return to faraway Europe. On boarding, we witness a space-time warp. While leaving from an African country, our passengers are all rigorously whiter than white. Their larger than wildlife look is what strikes us the most, though; it is as if all the 15th-century characters in the Flemish masters' paintings had decided to fly with us. In the Old Continent, such facial traits have long gone as have those supersized bodies. But, at the end of the day, what's the surprise? They still refer to this land as South Rhodesia...

So, without further ado, boarding is complete, and we'll soon reach the highest heavens. They all kindly greet each other. They all know one other; the exodus atmosphere is almost palpable. Perhaps, this is why on a route normally served by a humble 767 they decided to use a good old extra-large 747.

After take-off, the first service runs as smooth as silk, we finish it in a flash; long boring hours ahead of us before reaching London now. Night flights are often like that: after dinner, everybody falls asleep whilst us cabin crew, when not on our break, have to resist the temptation to fall into the arms of Morpheus while keeping up decent appearances, avoiding nodding off while walking or dribbling when standing. Faking wakefulness whilst fast asleep is an art that can be perfected over time and with a heavy load of jet lag under your belt.

Tonight, passengers are particularly sleepy. Not a soul around, their mouths are gaping maws frozen in noisy sounds, a few dancing dentures, the odd gold tooth gleaming in the darkness and the usual snoring. A routine cabin and toilet check and then, to kill time, the only thing left is the Daily Mail crosswords... soon to be interrupted.

A woman peeks from behind the curtains. A white head - just out of a Parisian coiffeur salon with silver curly hair in a fashionable hairdo - pops out of the crack. Ready for decapitation? The pussyfooting elderly lady is trying to tell us something, perhaps (and quite rightly) she is afraid of disturbing.

"Please, madam, do come in. How can we help? Do you care for a drink? A hot drink?" I ask with all the kindness still left in me at this ungodly hour.

"No, thanks."

But her face tells a completely different story, she is there for a reason, so we try to entice her with a snack.

"Look, we have tuck boxes; you can find savoury or sweet munchies. Come in and we'll show you."

"No, thanks," she answers still in the decapitation position from behind the curtained guillotine, as if she were a little kid hiding away after pulling a prank.

"Can I help you in any other way?"

"Yes," she whispers with some embarrassment.

"Feel free to tell us anything, we are here to help."

Before replying, she looks behind her back to make sure nobody is following her or is eavesdropping. She adjusts her impeccable mane, tucks her blouse in, rearranges the string of pearls around her neck, and looks up and then down; the light is too low to reveal a blush on her cheeks. In the end, she grasps the nettle and spills the beans. "You know the corridor at the back of the plane joining the two aisles, right?"

"Do you mean the one by the toilets?"

"Exactly! If I were you, I'd go and have a look… there are some youngsters, three to be precise, who… well, shouldn't be there… doing those things," she says and disappears after having dropped a bomb of that magnitude, swallowed up by the same darkness from which she had manifested.

We look at each other slightly dumbfounded. We could pretend it was a ghost but motivated by curiosity rather than by our resolve to restore law and order on board the aircraft, Mario and I decide to sweep the reported area. No need for words, just one look and we stomp like two wild elephants to announce our arrival in the hope that our military gait would command respect and strike terror.

We reach the back of the plane; we turn the corner behind the divider and who do we find? Two young fetching boys in their early twenties with their trousers down to their ankles and a kneeling damsel beseeching earthly pleasures and fighting a war on two fronts, at least at oral level. Our arrival does not seem to bother them in the least; the ménage à trois must go on… The damsel seems to act fairly and bestows equal zeal to both scions, giving them the same present with undivided attention.

We stomp our feet while standing, clear our voices to get their attention, but alas, we are invisible. Time to burst into action!

"Guys, come on, you just can't…" but the words choke in my throat. The damsel's reaction caches me by surprise. As she must have been taught since childhood, she makes sure she does not talk with a full mouth. Holding tightly to the forbidden fruits as if they were her mooring lines, she turns around and replies, "We are nearly there, almost finished!"

"What? Almost finished? You shouldn't even have started!" exclaims Mario.

They won't give up.

One of the two bachelors adds pompously, "We are all Oxford students (it beggars belief, what would the Cambridge ones do then?), we know perfectly well what we are doing!"

That's a good start! We are almost tempted to leave them in... her capable hands.

What has the world come to! Modesty and shame are not in fashion anymore. Audacity has always been mankind's companion since time immemorial, but what a cheek! If the youngsters don't stop, the protocol will have to be implemented. Our words can only achieve so much. Being the good, passionate, instinctive Latin boys that we are, we would like to disperse the threesome with a profane, 'Stop the hanky-panky, you dirty sods, shame on you! Get dressed and go back to your seats!' but the Anglo-Saxon etiquette follows a different rationale; any situation requires a specific procedure that must be applied and respected.

While Mario stays behind on... statuary watch (I wonder why), I run like hell to the flight deck, quickly explain what is happening at the other end of the plane to the captain. He has the authority to delegate to us special powers through a signed letter turning us into public officials. By the sparkly look in his eyes, he clearly holds back many questions he would like to ask about the girl's multitasking prowess, but duty comes first, and, given the seriousness of the events, he promptly issues the document so that I can rush back to the (ob)scene of the passionate crime. Nothing's changed, Mario has not even blinked by the looks of it! We have to follow the procedure and read out the document to the offenders.

I unfold it as if it were a royal edict, hoping it will achieve the intended effect and in front of the joyful I proclaim, "In the name of the Secretary of State of Her Britannic Majesty, I inform you that your behaviour represents an indecent act (Really?). We therefore urge you to stop immediately. If not, on arrival in London, you will be handed over to the authorities…"

I haven't even reached the bottom of the edict that the much-needed miracle happens, the young ones get unstuck, the boys cover up their modesties, the handmaid rises and composes herself adopting a Botticelli-style position and the three of them saunter back to their seats in the darkness, consigning their intimate encounter to oblivion.

Empty scene. All vanished! Mario and I look at each other in disbelief.

Is life a dream or do dreams help us live a better life?

48

One Job, Many Hats

"No, the duty-free bag is too small; go and get the green recycling liner, and while you are there, get a couple of extension seatbelts, do you mind?"

How is it possible that I need to get a shoe from First Class because my colleague Linette says that both shoes won't fit in the fore wardrobe?

"Place them on a shoetree because sometimes my ankles swell up inflight," orders the Babylonian ziggurat sitting in 1A, a 7-foot colossus with such huge hands and feet who could be easily mistaken for a telamon.

Since I can't go through the cabin with that humongous smelly log, I try to put the ogre's footwear (Cinderella could have comfortably slept in it) in the liner and squeeze it in the Business Class wardrobe. The size of that foot grotto is quite amazing, but the hole for the ankle is... breath-taking. A dwarf baobab could easily grow in it. With my botanical doubt in mind and after having sorted out that megalithic shoe, I go back to Economy where till five minutes before it was all hunky-dory.

"My husband is diabetic," says with an attitude the passenger sitting by Door 3 left. "The problem is that he has forgotten his syringes. And by the way, he is also insulin dependent," carries on the cantankerous woman.

"Don't worry, I need my injection at midday, but I can always use my pills," he retorts, giving her a dirty look.

"WHICH PILLS??? Go on, show him the jar of your half-eaten pills!"

I recover instantly from the giant puss-in-boots shock, now it's time to change hat, and I turn into Dr Kildare. I inspect the jar of pills that the diabetic's wife throws into my hands... I see... not one single pill is actually intact, they are all half-eaten, as if they were termite-infested Smarties.

"You see? He tastes them, doesn't like them and puts them back in the jar. And back he goes to the doctor to have new ones prescribed. I always tell him that they are not sweets, but he is so stubborn! Mulish, really! This will teach him a lesson, because now pills are no longer enough, and he needs to inject himself in the tummy. But guess what! Today, of all days, he has forgotten his syringes!"

"This could be a problem, ma'am. Let's see if there is anything we can do while we are still on the ground."

"Do whatever you like, but I have already put on my onesie and I'm not going anywhere, I won't get off!"

I speak with the cabin manager and the captain. They unanimously decide to have him offloaded and rebooked on the next flight.

Easier said than done... who is going to break the news to him... them?

"WHAT??? When we get home, I'll kill her, it's all her fault!" shouts the neurodiabetic while his wife collects all their belongings getting ready to disembark.

"By the way, I could have drunk it; I don't need a syringe to get my insulin fix!" he grunts while walking through the cabin heading towards the exit door in his onesie.

Bottoms up!

Emergency over, Dr Kildare can hang up his stethoscope.

Later on. Mid Atlantic.

"Your job must be so amazing!" confesses to me a smiling passenger while I'm trying to eat a bite before going for my break.

"Above all, it's very varied, no two flights are the same," I answer suspiciously.

What hat will I have to wear now? On this flight, I have already been a shoemaker in First, a diabetologist in Economy, what now?

"I have eight weeks," she says apocalyptically.

"To do what?" I ask her. Lost my appetite for food. Ready for a revelation.

"I MUST lose at least two and a half stones in two months, and then I MUST also learn French… in eight weeks as well," she admits holding her head in her hands. "I take two laxatives a day; I swear, everything that goes in comes out; I sleep with my earbuds on listening 24/7 to my French Rosetta Stone course. Surely, something must be going in, innit? What d'ya reckon? Will I be able to make it? I've always wanted to become a stewardess for this airline, and I will not be stopped by a few extra pounds... at the moment I spend my life shuttling from the bathroom to my study, sometimes I even take three laxatives a day and I end up studying on the throne. It's a pity, because everything else is perfect. I have already passed my swimming and aptitude tests. I just need to go back, they want to check on my weight and see if I have improved my French, just a little. But believe you me, it's already good enough. Last time I didn't know the difference between *pourquoi* and *parce-que*. It's not that bad, innit? Got any tips for me?"

I understand, it's time to wear my Freudian hat, but this time I am the one who wants to lie down on the chaise longue. Don't you dare analyse me; I just want to rest!

49

New Update Available

"...one must know the world in all its aspects. Variety is the spice of life, after all. We must refrain from jumping to conclusions or having tunnel vision!" This is the farewell sentence that concludes our third and last day of a refresher course for cabin crew who have been off work for more than 180 days for all different kinds of reasons: maternity/paternity, unpaid leave, life-rethink break... I feel as if my knowledge gap has been filled, now I can go back flying with renewed confidence; I have the tools to tackle any celestial or terrestrial hidden danger.

Some useful must-knows I've learned today:

1. In Tibet you need a licence to reincarnate
2. Striptease is illegal in Iceland
3. In Iran, men are banned from sporting Western hair styles, especially ponytails and too much hair gel
4. In Saudi Arabia and Pakistan, it is illegal to celebrate Valentine's Day in public
5. In Rome, keeping a goldfish in a bowl is not allowed
6. In Greece, stilettoes are forbidden while visiting archaeological sites
7. In Indonesia and Saudi Arabia, onanism is illegal
8. In Germany, you are not allowed to stop on an Autobahn
9. In Russia, Belarus and Kazakhstan, it is illegal to wear lace underwear in public

10. In Florida, married women cannot go skydiving on a Sunday
11. In Thailand, walking down the street without knickers is banned
12. In Switzerland, it is illegal to flush a toilet after 22.00
13. In Portugal, peeing in the ocean is forbidden
14. In Japan, Vicks Vaporub is outlawed
15. In Singapore, chewing gums are illegal

Crickey! I can't remember what I'm not supposed to do in Barbados!

All this knowledge is really liberating (or rather prevents you from losing your freedom or ending up in trouble) and makes you a world traveller, a true citizen of the world! Now I know what to pack in my suitcase...

But this was a quiz... I don't know why 90% of attendees thought the flushing ban applied to Venice.

Anyway, I feel ready for the big wide world once again. I'll spread my wings and polish my halo; tomorrow I'm due to fly to Trumpland...

I don't know why; I can't stop thinking about the young woman from Ealing... she would definitely be in trouble somewhere!

50

Angelina

In any airline, thousands of cabin crew must interact with new colleagues and passengers daily. But where is this bond, such team spirit, created with people you've never seen before and with whom you must spend the next ten, eleven, twelve hours of your life in close proximity while attending to a load of punters not always having realistic expectations?

In briefing rooms around the world in fifteen minutes max. What happens and is said is highly confidential. Normally, after a short introduction, the in-charge crew member, a role that goes under a plethora of names depending on the airline, asks individual or group technical questions – known in jargon as SEP (safety and emergency procedures) check – to comply with CAA (Civil Aviation Authority) requirements. This is then followed by some more commercial stuff, including a short discussion of the passenger list which is often accompanied by some sort of useful comments by the ground staff highlighting special requests, issues, peculiarities or some more down-to-earth remarks such as 'no alcohol', 'nervous flyer', 'keeps asking for an upgrade', 'might smoke', etc. So, you get the general picture, and you might choose in which cabin to work according to your skills and mood of the day. It is also true that some working positions are chosen according to seniority or your personal predisposition. Sometimes, this can cause problems. Just imagine if a colleague who at home likes a drink or two, on board ends up serving a proverbial drunkard and succumbs to Stockholm Syndrome! A recipe for disaster.

Each cabin manager has his/her personal technique to break the ice, to build a close-knit winning team. Some colleagues swear to have witnessed a Ring-a-round the rosie (as they call it on the other side of the Pond), group hugging, pub-style quizzes etc. All for the sake of creating a bond!

"Close the door!" our cabin manager instructs Janine. "Before becoming cabin crew, each one of you was something or, in some cases, someone else. I'd like each of you to share with us a curious fact from your past."

Fourteen lives, all somehow interesting in their own ways, randomly chosen by fate to operate this flight to Los Angeles.

Four of them really strike me.

"I was a magistrate, also known as justice of peace," Jennifer says.

"I was a medium for Scotland Yard," Siobhan admits.

"I used to be a French teacher at college," Paul reveals.

"I was a model," Becky shows off.

"Very good. Now that we know a little better what kind of past expertise we can count on, in the few minutes we have left, before pilots come in, I'd like to share with you a brief anecdote. As you know, today we are flying on a 747, registration number GB - XXXX. Why am I telling you this? Obviously, not to scare you off," he says half-jokingly. "But to get you ready to think out of the box, not the black one!"

"This is what happened a few years back on GB - XXXX. On a flight back to London from Johannesburg, one of our colleagues, let's call her Joanne, was on her break; but since she wasn't particularly sleepy, she was sitting downstairs in our rest area, reading a book. A passenger opened the door, THE door that should always be locked as you all know! Joanne apologised, told her that was a 'crew only' area and, thinking she was looking for the loo, pointed her in the right direction. But the lady said it wasn't what she was looking for and asked her to take care of her husband sitting in 54D, to bring him a Baccardi&Coke, his favourite drink, and to tell him not to worry about her.

"The lady then left; Joanne fell asleep. We all know how important our rest is on a long-haul flight, don't we? When she went back from her break, she suddenly remembered the incident, took a Bacardi&Coke to the gentleman, told him that his wife had asked for it and apologised for the delay. 'Impossible,' he said. 'My wife Angelina is on board, but in the hold unfortunately, in a coffin. I'm taking her back home and then to Paris where she wished to be buried. Is this some kind of sick joke or what?' he spat visibly upset. Joanne described the lady she saw to him. 'This is the way I dressed her for her last journey. How dare you!' he said."

Well, my break is ruined, but this is really an incredible story!

"Really strange! Look, I've got goosebumps," says Siobhan, our medium colleague. "While you were telling the story, I channelled a message. Change of identity. New Life. Sorry but sometimes I get these messages but I don't know what I'm talking about!"

Now, I'm told that in any respectable company there is a haunting story going around, narrated slightly differently every time it's shared…

Knock, knock.

"May we come in?" the pilots ask.

"Of course, we've just finished our briefing; have you got anything to add?"

"Yes, we don't know if we're going today, there is a slight technical issue. Our engineers need to replace a small part, but at the moment they can't find a spare. The flight is likely to be cancelled. Just wait around for further instructions."

Oh God, forgive them because sometimes they don't know what they are talking about, especially when promising smooth flights...

And an hour later we take to the skies. Here we are, on board our lovely and cosy 747, registration number GB-XXXX though!

Somewhere over the Atlantic.

"I went into the cockpit as usual to serve the boys their meals... but now I can't find it!" tells me Becky, my upper-deck colleague.

"What have you lost?"

"My passport! But I haven't lost it!"

"But why did you have your passport with you on the flight deck?"

"I always carry it with me, everywhere. I keep it in the pocket of my gilet. I feel safe that way. I don't understand," she says worryingly.

"Well, but are you..." I say, but she interrupts me.

"I mean, I'm famous for having left quite a few things on the cockpit, willingly or unwillingly… bras, G-strings… you name it! I must admit, I might have been a bit of a flying mattress in my heyday; God forbid, never a cart tart, though, don't get me wrong, luv!" she adds with a smirk. "But it's never happened to me before that they take my passport! I feel naked without it," she concludes.

Becky, I must admit, you have a most peculiar sense of shame.

While Helen of Troy caused the launch of a thousand ships, Becky of Liverpool must have fired up more than a cockpit with her antics. Rumour has it that a fight broke out on a flight when three passengers claimed to have Becky's real phone number. A gentleman from the Middle East bought the entire content of the duty-free trolley in an attempt to win her heart. But why in the skies would anyone steal her passport?

Three hours later.

"Has anyone left their passport under the pillow in bunk number 5?" Paul asks.

"I think it might be Becky's; she's been looking for it everywhere!" I say.

"But I did NOT put it under my pillow when I went for my break! Someone is having me on!" she protests.

Angelinaaa.

She opens her passport and flicks through the pages. "I didn't have a stamp of the Eiffel Tower on my passport! Who did this?" Becky grumbles.

Angelina, where are you? Are you having fun?

We land in Los Angeles.

On the coach bound for our hotel. Darkness. Curtains drawn. Smell of throbbing feet that have worked for the last eleven hours. A few crew members already dribbling away. A phone goes off, a strange ringtone, it sounds like *La Marseillaise*, the French national anthem. Nobody answers it.

Allons enfants de la patrieee…

The phone carries on ringing.

"Becky, isn't that your bag? Why are you not picking up?" Siobhan asks.

"Yes, it's my bag, but I've never had that flipping ringtone!" she answers.

Angelina, why Becky?

"It's obvious that she's trying to get a message through to you. Something to do with your identity, maybe the need to change your life," adds our former medium colleague.

"I'm definitely not picking up! And by the way, tonight, I shall NOT sleep alone!"

The pilots immediately turn round like hunting moray eels, their eyes brimming with hope.

"Not you! It's all change from now on!" Becky remarks.

Angelina, happy now?

Printed in Great Britain
by Amazon